Snapshots: First publish

Copyright for the individual pie
and they assert the moral right

Porch Dreaming Copyright © 2011 Elsa Halling
Cutting Grass Copyright © 2014 Derek Miller
Gecko Copyright © 2013 Di de Wolfson
An Uncomfortable Silence Copyright © 2014 Mike Watkinson
Sister Francis Copyright © 2014 Maidy Clark
The River Copyright © 2013 Peter Smerdon
His Bag for Life Copyright © 2014 Penny McCulloch
Dating with Animals Copyright © 2014 Derek Miller
Trish and Chips Copyright © 2013 Paul Chiswick
Friends Reunited Copyright © 2014 Maidy Clark
A Poor Do Copyright © 2013 Elsa Halling
Orange Copyright © 2014 Di de Wolfson
Florence and Bill Copyright © 2014 Katrina Ritters
13 Weston Road Copyright © 2014 Cashel Brook
See No Evil Copyright © 2014 Mark Bradbury
Sandra. RIP Copyright © 2014 Kay Howles
The Sergeant's Speech Copyright © 2014 Derek Miller
A Special Visit Copyright © 2014 Dave Griffiths
The Big Issue Copyright © 2013 Paul Chiswick
The Reunion Copyright © 2013 Anne Santos
Wait Inside Copyright © 2014 Di de Wolfson
The Advisor's Atonement Copyright © 2013 Paul Chiswick
An Heir for Pemberley Copyright © 2013 Elsa Halling
No Plan Made Copyright © 2014 Kay Howles
Promise Copyright © 2012 Peter Smerdon
The Doctor's Graveyard Copyright © 2013 Mike Watkinson
The Dream Copyright © 2014 Maggie Cabeza
H_2O Copyright © 2014 Di de Wolfson
The Letter Copyright © 2014 Maidy Clark

All rights reserved. No part of this publication may be reproduced, stored in a retrieval system, or transmitted, in any form or by any means, electronic, mechanical, photocopying, recording or otherwise, without the prior permission of Balsall Writers.

All characters in this publication are fictitious and any resemblance to real persons, living or dead, is purely coincidental.

ISBN 978 1501006234

Contents

Porch Dreaming	Elsa Halling	**1**
Cutting Grass	Derek Miller	**11**
Gecko	Di de Wolfson	**18**
An Uncomfortable Silence	Mike Watkinson	**19**
Sister Francis	Maidy Clark	**26**
The River	Peter Smerdon	**31**
His Bag for Life	Penny McCulloch	**40**
Dating with Animals	Derek Miller	**42**
Trish and Chips	Paul Chiswick	**50**
Friends Reunited	Maidy Clark	**55**
A Poor Do	Elsa Halling	**61**
Orange	Di de Wolfson	**70**
Florence and Bill	Katrina Ritters	**72**
13 Weston Road	Cashel Brook	**77**
See No Evil	Mark Bradbury	**87**
Sandra. RIP	Kay Howles	**93**
The Sergeant's Speech	Derek Miller	**98**
A Special Visit	Dave Griffiths	**100**
The Big Issue	Paul Chiswick	**110**
The Reunion	Anne Santos	**112**
'Wait Inside'	Di de Wolfson	**117**
The Advisor's Atonement	Paul Chiswick	**119**
An Heir for Pemberley	Elsa Halling	**128**
No Plan Made	Kay Howles	**137**
Promise	Peter Smerdon	**139**
The Doctor's Graveyard	Mike Watkinson	**148**
The Dream	Maggie Cabeza	**160**
H$_2$O	Di de Wolfson	**165**
The Letter	Maidy Clark	**167**
About the authors		

Snapshots

An Anthology

Balsall Writers

Introduction

As one of the founders of Balsall Writers in 2011 I believe that words are our most powerful weapon; they are the tools of life.

Whether we speak or write in anger, in love, in business, in prayer or as authors, words shape lives, words teach and words live long after their creator is dead.

Without words we would be nothing, so really "words are all we have"; they are our most precious gift, whether written or said, mimed or drawn, words communicate and make us human.

We are Wordsmiths creating, enjoying words as our craft. We respect and embrace words using them to try and convey that incident, that moment as we arrange and re-arrange, delete and add, despair and rejoice as we create in poetry or prose.

So words written as texts, as blogs, as books, as letters – giving you a name at the beginning of life, leaving your worth at the end of life and in between, words of love or grief – words give "SNAPSHOTS" of moments in your life.

So this is our anthology of words splattered on paper by members of our three groups, to create interest, amusement and enjoyment.

Anne Santos
Chair, 2014
Balsall Writers

Porch Dreaming

Elsa Halling

When the sun paints the evening sky with the soft pearly tones of pink and gold and mauve and the labour of the day is done, then comes the time for dreaming. The time to sit on the front porch, sip coffee, fill a clay pipe with tobacco and watch the kaleidoscope of colours in the sky. To see shapes in the clouds, shapes which could be grand sail boats voyaging to foreign shores; boats that would sail to freedom.

Biddie didn't have those fantasies any more. Those were the dreams of youth, dreams they all had in the old days before the war came. She rocked gently in the battered old chair, the smoke from her pipe drifting slowly skyward, making its own ethereal swirls in the fading light. For Biddie it should now be a time for reflection, for remembrance and relaxation, but tonight it could be none of those things; she carried too much anxiety for the future. Not for her own future, she would end her days as they had begun, on a plantation. Not the one where she grew up, but the one where she found work and a home after the war. The Randolphs gave her shelter and employment when she arrived in the area with Fern. They had never asked questions about her past life, nor queried Fern's ancestry. The child's paler skin told them all they needed to know. First she had been a house maid in the Randolph plantation house, then, as the children arrived she became a nanny to the next generations. She had helped raise the master's children and then his grandchildren. Now, with the little house and patch of dirt she had struggled hard to pay for, she felt more secure than she had ever been. Porch time was now a time for chewing over problems and sometimes, if her thoughts drifted along the right pathways, solving them. Tonight she had to find a solution to the problem that was Ruby.

The great orb of the sun sunk lower creating fire on the horizon. Biddie's pipe had gone out. Leaning forward she tapped the bowl of the pipe on the porch rail, making sure the ash fell onto the bare dirt beyond. She leaned back in her old wicker chair, its cushions had moulded to the shape of her body over the years, and her eyelids drooped. In that state between waking and sleeping the image of a little girl seemed clear to Biddie. The child was drawing pictures in the dust of the yard and called out to her, 'Look Nana, I've drawn a chook. Come and see!' And her younger self had stepped nimbly down from the porch and looked at the child's drawing. 'Why, child I can see feathers and all!' she'd praised Fern's efforts.

Fern had always been a secretive little girl, hiding simple treasures she found around the plantation, like the shiny smooth pebbles she picked up when paddling in the creek. She enjoyed hiding from Biddie and the other children, appearing from her secret places to startle her mother when she searched for her at sundown. She grew into a secretive teenager, who, when her work in the house was done, would disappear for the whole evening, never saying where she had been or how she had spent her time. Fern had worked hard at school and Biddie had hopes of her becoming a teacher. But she had learnt the foolishness of having hopes about the future. "Sufficient unto the day" had to be her motto now.

Biddie stirred restlessly, as a heavy sadness seeped through her bones. Whatever had become of that little girl so proud of the chicken she had drawn in the dirt? Her eyelids flickered and she glanced across the field to the back of the big house and to the door that opened off one end of it; the door that led to the old parsons' room. All the plantation houses had one. They accommodated an itinerant parson who could spend the night between his travels from one settlement to another, and, arriving late would not disturb the family by having to go inside the main house. Often, in the old days, she would come up to the big house early in the morning from her own home, and find the room occupied by some preacher or other who had left it too late to complete his journey. That room, she was sure, was the source of all the troubles.

As a child Fern had enjoyed helping Biddie to take coffee and cornbread to the occasional occupants of the parsons' room. It usually happened on the first Monday morning of the month, when a visiting parson was returning home after preaching in one of the churches in the locality. When Fern had grown a little older Biddie felt it best to do the job alone, but one Monday there had been an emergency in the big house. One of the Randolph children was sick and Biddie was needed to help, so Fern had taken in the coffee and cornbread by herself.

A few months later, when Fern had just turned sixteen, Biddie noticed the girl was developing a thickening waistline. Realising the reason for it Biddie questioned her daughter, 'Who's the daddy? Who's you bin wid child?' she had asked; angrily at first, then sadly. As far as Biddie was aware, pretty as Fern was, there had been no boys sniffing around her. Was this to be the fate of every young negro woman, barely out of childhood? 'Who did this to you girl?' She questioned Fern again and again, but the girl's lips remained tightly sealed. Porch talk amongst the local folks yielded no information either. No one in the neighbourhood had any gossip about Fern to pass on to Biddie, and they would have been quick enough to do so if there had been anything to tell. The local men were eager to hunt the culprit down, but Fern had remained stubbornly silent about the paternity of her unborn child.

So it was that Ruby entered the world in the little house her mother had been brought to as an infant. A healthy, noisy baby whom Biddie had immediately fallen in love with and had put aside her anger with Fern. What the mother had done weren't no fault of the child, she reasoned to herself. 'Cos she's born out of wedlock ain't sufficient reason not to love her,' she'd told her daughter. But within a week Fern had gone, disappeared like a dream in the night. Biddie had expected her to come home after a few days, but since that morning, such a short time after Ruby's birth, she had neither seen nor heard of her. It was if she had never existed.

By the time Ruby was just a few months old it became apparent that her father could not be from the black community. Ruby's skin was lighter even than her mother's; it was the colour of the honey Biddie collected from the bee hives which stood beneath the pear trees. As she grew out of infancy her soft black hair was wavy rather than the tight corkscrew curls of her grandmother's. Her eyes were the colour of the grey-green marbles she liked to play with. It was then that Biddie had her suspicions about Ruby's paternity. 'Your daddy must be one o' dem parsons,' she had told the baby as she rocked her to sleep.

In the swirl of Biddie's dreams Fern's childish face transformed into that of Ruby's. Ruby had liked to draw in the dirt as her mother had done. Mrs Randolph had persuaded Biddie that Ruby should be raised with her own grandchildren and so Ruby had grown up alongside the four Randolph children, unaware of any differences between them. Mrs Randolph had given her clothes her grandchildren had grown out of and tied ribbons in her hair. Biddie remembered the difficulties this had caused from time to time. Ruby would come home from school telling of how Mayrella had taunted her about living with the white folks, and giving herself airs and graces.

As the glowing embers died out of the sky and the grey shadows became faded shapes in the darkening sky, a cooling breeze teased Biddie's skirts. She shivered and pulled an old patchwork shawl from the back of her chair, her "rainbow shawl", Ruby had always called it. As she shrugged it around her shoulders a sigh escaped from deep within her. She had to make sure Ruby's life would be better than her mother's; she must make plans before it was too late. She must stop the canker that was becoming the black woman's destiny.

Ruby was a dreamer, and dreams could lead to trouble. Biddie knew that only too well. Black folk still could not afford the luxury of dreams. Biddie's life had not been easy, but she knew it had been a lot easier than some black folks. In other households women servants had been turned out if they found themselves with child, but without a husband. Fornication was as great a sin as murder in the narrow minds of some of the plantation owners. Biddie had no time for religion, especially when she thought of Fern and what had happened to her. That parson she had taken coffee to had never shown his face at the Big House again. Biddie wondered if he ever knew he had a daughter. Perhaps she judged him too harshly and even now he was taking care of Fern. But she thought not. What would a white preacher man want with a black wife? She tried to feel less harshly about him; if he hadn't married Fern then perhaps he was employing her. She liked to think this might be the case; it brought comfort to her in the middle of the night when visions of what might have become of her daughter taunted her sleepless soul.

Biddie stirred in her chair and gazed up at the sky. The sun had disappeared completely and the light from a thin sliver of waning moon was creating a faint dappled pattern on the dirt beneath the oak trees. Biddie rose from her chair and shuffled indoors to refill her coffee mug from the pot she had left to keep hot on the stove. She swallowed some of the bitter liquid and considered staying in the house. But the call of the porch was too great, it was too soon to take to her bed, and besides she needed to watch for Ruby who was looking after the younger Randolph children. Especially now, after what she had seen that afternoon; she must make sure that Ruby came straight home and didn't wander off into the night.

Ruby had spent most of that afternoon sitting beneath the pear tree that grew beside the lane that led down to the cotton fields. Biddie had looked out at her from time to time while she was making hoecakes to have with fried chicken for their supper. But once she had taken them out of the oven and put them to cool on the windowsill she had sat down to rest in the chair by the open window. She was weary after her efforts, and the now regular ache in her side demanded she rest. The sultry afternoon heat and her tiredness invited sleep to overtake her as it did so often these days. Her rest was disturbed by murmuring voices in the yard outside. She could hear Ruby's tones, a light and teasing cadence, interspersed with a deeper, masculine voice. At first she thought it was part of the dream she had been enjoying. The dream in which Ruby was accepting her diploma from high school and preparing to go to college to train as a teacher, as she had so wanted for her mother. The low voices continued and Biddie was thoroughly roused from her sleep, realising that the voices were not part of any dream.

She eased her old body out of the chair and stood by the window. There was Ruby, no longer supine beneath the pear tree, but standing in the arms of that no-good Jimmy Wilson, who was kissing her ardently. Biddie hadn't been able to help herself. 'Ruby!' she had called out, not in reproof but in despair. The two figures sprang apart. Ruby glanced across and caught Biddie's eye, then looked quickly away. But brash Jimmy Wilson gave her a wide grin and a cheeky wave, then whistling, sauntered off along the lane to the shack he lived in with his numerous siblings and worn-out mother. Jimmy was the eldest of the brood and should by now be working to help his mother rear his brothers and sisters. Since his father had died in a drunken brawl the family often went hungry. Biddie liked Sunny Wilson, his mother, God knows she had little to feel sunny about these days, or any day for that matter, but she had no intention of Ruby hooking up with that family. She had worked hard these last years to make sure Ruby could do better for herself than that.

Ruby had come into the house as if nothing had happened. 'Ruby, what's you bin doin'? How long you bin letting that Jimmy Wilson kiss you like that?' Biddie had been reproachful rather than angry. Ruby made out that that had been the first time, and 'He din't mean nothin' by it.' Now this had made her angry, for in Biddie's experience no man ever means "nothing" when he kisses a girl like Ruby. She had shouted at her granddaughter and slapped her face angrily, but was instantly remorseful when she saw the tears in Ruby's eyes.

Absentmindedly Biddie rubbed the ache in her side and pondered on how she ought to have handled the matter. Would it have been better if she hadn't gotten angry? But a woman can't help her feelings, and disappointment had washed through her; she could see all her hard work and brave hopes for Ruby dissolve in the lingering moments of that kiss. Fully awake now, Biddie resolved to get Ruby married before any harm could come to her. But it would never be to Jimmy Wilson, she had to do better than that.

Last Sunday, after church she had had an unusual conversation with Enoch Lambert. Ruby had sung a solo during the service that morning and afterwards, outside the church, he had complimented Biddie on how well she had brought up young Ruby. 'She's a credit to you to be sure,' he'd said, 'she'll make any man proud to be her husband. ' And had given her a very knowing look. At the time Biddie had scoffed to herself at the idea of Ruby married to a man like Enoch Lambert. To be sure he was a good man, but Ruby was going to go to college and be a teacher before she had any thoughts of marriage, wasn't she? But what she had seen this afternoon was making her change her mind. Perhaps Enoch Lambert with his sixty acres of decent farmland would be the answer to her problem. The more Biddie thought about it the more she liked the idea. Enoch Lambert's place was only a mile outside the village, so she would be able to see Ruby regularly and, God-willing, would live to see great-grandchildren too. This thought soothed her unquiet mind. Brother Lambert would not have been Biddie's first choice for Ruby; he was old enough to be her father, but he had taken good care of his wife before she died, and she was sure he would look after Ruby too. For too many years the black woman had been at the bottom of the heap, and Biddie was determined it would be different for her granddaughter.

The evening was drawing on, and as a cloud cleared from the face of the moon a silver gleam fell onto the porch where Biddie was sitting. It lit up her lined face and also her spirit. She now felt sure she had the answer to all her troubles. Brother Lambert was a man who never came straight to the point and always tested the ground before putting forward his ideas. But Biddie knew him well and was quite satisfied that in his roundabout way he had been making a play for Ruby. Now she was impatient for Ruby's return. She must not delay, not just for Ruby's sake but for her own. The pain in her side had become more persistent these last months; it could not auger anything good, maybe great-grandchildren was a dream too far for her. Drawing her shawl tightly around her shoulders

Biddie went to fetch some more coffee. She didn't want to fall asleep and have Ruby sneak into the house without waking her. Sitting on the porch she had come to a solution to the problem; Ruby must accept it too, and the sooner it was done the easier Biddie would feel.

The moon had shifted high in the sky to the far side of the pear trees before the sound of voices from the Big House disturbed Biddie's contentment. She looked across and could pick out, sashaying across the dirt, the light blur that was Ruby in her pale blue cotton frock. Ruby liked herself in that frock; she said it set off her honey coloured skin. Yes, that girl was definitely ready for a husband Biddie convinced herself.

'Why you waited up Nana?' asked Ruby when she reached the porch. 'You know Missus Randolph always watches to see me safe home.'

Biddie patted the second chair on the porch, 'Come and sit beside me, Ruby, we's got things to settle afore we sleep.'

Cutting Grass

Derek Miller

Simpson casually left her bike leaning on a fence. Her new uniform felt comfortable. She walked confidently into the crime scene. Getting in was easy, no lock on the gate. Security was generally not an issue in this area. She stood and surveyed the large back garden. It was a hot, dry, August day. There had been no rain for months. The grass was green, - green and short. In this heat the masses of flowers were wilting slightly. Numerous birds could be heard in the trees. She walked around. Crouching down she touched the lawn, - it felt damp. A well-tended vegetable patch was overflowing with brightly coloured beans. There was a sickly smell of freshly cut grass. In the corner by the house was a washing line with clothes. She noted for a man and a woman. She could see the stripes on the lawn. There were stripes in the grass. She felt her thoughts explode, mentally counting the lines.

There was a sudden crash as the back door flew open. 'What are you doing here?' followed by a short, dark haired woman who appeared on the path.

She stopped her mental arithmetic and turned round; 'I'm Higher Constable Simpson.'

'Hello, I'm Helen Jones and this is my house.'

Simpson was tall, blond and svelte, and looked down at Helen. Simpson noticed with some disdain the use of makeup, and what must have been dye as her hair was all one colour. As a good party colleague she would never waste environmental resources on vanity products. The way Jones was moving suggested she didn't exercise much either. Her clothes showed how difficult it was to dress well. There were no shops in these outlying areas.

'What's going on here?' asked Simpson.

'Nothing much, there's not much to do. A lot of the houses are empty and no one wants to move here out of the city.'

'Are you going to tell me?'

'There's not a lot to tell. On most days I see the woman from a few doors down, Marge, she's my best friend. There's nothing else to do. Since the bloody green dictators put in petrol rationing and stopped the bus service on supposedly environmental grounds we've been virtually cut off.'

'Don't insult the Eco Party. If it wasn't for them this planet would have died years ago. We need to sort out the mess left by years of over consumption. And don't insult me, look at this.' Simpson stood up straight, folded her arms and looked at Jones.

'Oh I don't think it looks that bad, considering the summer we've had. There's no shops round here to buy anything nice for the garden. We're lucky if a van with basic groceries comes round once a month. He missed the last two months so we're living on what we can get from the garden.' Helen looked around and started to fidget. She started to move towards the house.

Simpson was standing in the middle of the lawn. 'Don't try going there, I've been very patient so far, but this is enough. What's going on here?'

Helen started again, 'There's not much that goes....'

'The grass – it's short and green,' interrupted Simpson.

'It's that sort, keeps its colour and doesn't need cutting.'

'Rubbish, you've been seen cutting it, and there's damp so it must have been watered.'

'Who's seen me cutting it, was it that nosey woman up the road who's just arrived in the village?'

'Never you mind, you've been rumbled.'

'Oh come on, no, it's my first time. Why don't you go after real criminals, like the ones that stole my chickens last week? I reported it but nothing happened.'

'As long as they didn't contravene the law on fuel usage then there's no crime to consider.' Simpson stared at her. 'What do you mean about the new arrival? There shouldn't be anyone moving to the village. It's not in our long term plan.'

'So now we've both said something we shouldn't. What's your long term plan?'

'It's nothing for you to worry your little head about.'

'Don't be so patronising, I could be your mother, and I bet you wouldn't speak to her like that.'

'And don't you bring my mother into this conversation. If she wasn't already dead I'd have her committed if she behaved like you.'

'I'm sorry to hear about your mother, and I wasn't being disrespectful to her, only commenting on your attitude.'

'Okay let's move on from this. There's still the question of you cutting the grass. This contravenes so many laws on wasting energy, releasing carbon back into the atmosphere and being totally unnecessary. You've also watered the grass. You know the laws on wasting water.'

Simpson turned round as she heard the sound. The door opened and out shuffled an old man. 'Who's he?' She resisted the temptation to ask how the corpse moved.

'Can I introduce Andrew, my husband.'

He slowly moved from side to side and made his way towards them. In a very hesitant and stammering manner he said, 'Hello.'

Helen came and held his hand. 'You've probably realised by now that Andrew has Parkinson's disease. There are no treatments or medicines, everything is deemed environmentally unsustainable. So he's left here with me.'

Simpson was just about to say the party line about drugs being so wasteful. The raw materials used to make drugs, compared to the benefits. But then she looked at him and remembered her own father. She had only been in the force a year when her father was diagnosed with Parkinson's. He had deteriorated quickly. Her mother was in favour of getting drugs on the black market. But Simpson had said that this was so against environmental considerations that she couldn't. She was a good party member. Looking after her father put so much strain on her mother that she died soon after he did.

'Why did you want to cut the grass?'

'Next week it's the village golf tournament and it will be Andrew's last chance to play. Probably will be the last golf match here, as there are so few people left. So I wanted shorter grass so he could practice his putting. Also we like to sit out here enjoying the garden. Those interfering new people don't seem to like us.'

'I'm going to find out about these newcomers; where do they live?'

'Just across the road, number 40. You can't miss it, it's the only one occupied in that block.'

'Stay here, I'll be back.'

Simpson walked purposely towards the house. She was thinking over half the people in the village had already left. Remaining was a ghost, run-down buildings, a memory that should be erased. There must not be anyone new moving into any of the homes. Houses were left to deteriorate. There were no new services. It may not be long before the village was completely deserted and could revert back to woodland. People living there were left to their own devices and only crimes against the environment would be investigated. The village was in Simpson's patch, but she was an infrequent visitor. She didn't like the long cycle ride here. Often she had to mend a puncture. The old roads had deteriorated to dirt tracks with sharp stones.

Knocking on the door she shouted 'Hello.'

A young couple appeared at the door. They were carrying backpacks and wearing cycling shorts.

'Hello.'

'I'm HC Simpson investigating eco crimes. What are you doing here?'

'I'm Steve and this is Claire. We're clearing out some old bits from my grandparent's house. It's for my mother she's got dementia and we hoped that some of the items would help bring back her memory. It was my father's idea, as you know there are no pills she can take.'

'How long are you here for?'

'We're leaving today. On our bikes, it's a long way back to the bus route. At one time we were promised that we could inherit the family home. But with the plans to run down the estates and new laws prohibiting sole occupation of land that won't be possible.'

'Don't push your luck too much. Did you phone the eco report line about the old couple who live just down the road, at number 47?'

'No it wasn't us. We want to be out of here quickly, and let other people live how they want to.'

'Okay, in that case just get on your way.'

Simpson walked back and sat on a crumbling wall next to her bike. She took a drink. In this case she knew what she should do. Put a restraining clamp on Helen so she couldn't move out of the house for six months and commit any further crimes. This was the party line. So that she would have to rely on the goodwill of neighbours to bring food. This often only lasted a few weeks. She knew the overall plan which was to close down these uneconomic villages and move everyone into the utopia of shared energy, efficient accommodation.

After her mother died she moved to the flats, described as the ideal living accommodation. It was clean basic and designed to be environmentally friendly. Basic was the word. You moved floors based on how many stairs you could climb. Changing so often that she had few personal possessions left. The lower floors were a bit derelict as the flats were often broken into. There would be a sharing of anything useful. The Eco Party had put in new laws on joint ownership of goods. She looked round at these old derelict houses. At least Helen and Andrew had each other. When she got old there would be no-one to look after her. She knew what she had to do.

She went back to number 47. 'Hello Helen.'

'How did you get on, Simpson?'

'In this case I'm going to cycle back and say there was no crime. Count yourself lucky, and don't do it again.'

'No I won't, thank you very much.'

Simpson moved towards her bike. She didn't look back, there was nothing she could say and next year they wouldn't be there.

Gecko

Di deWolfson

Cool feet set you at a jaunty angle,
a whip of muscular sand sculpted
across a slab of white wall,
holding my attention, daring me to
blink and miss your tongue
slicking over dusty amber eyes.

More certainly than any star
you fix my far-from-home position,
strange comforter exposed on
this white-wash, as I am white
against a sundried landscape.

By morning you are camouflaged
your belly warmed on a feast of insects
lured by the radiance of my blood.

By evening I will have lost contact
with the ground, relying on properties
only partially grasped, envying your
full-bodied faith in the vertical.

An Uncomfortable Silence

Mike Watkinson

David Willis was sweating. Profusely. Silently.

Greene's parody of Descartes – 'I feel discomfort, therefore I am alive' – brought no relief. An hour ago (or was it two?) he had had some shade from a baobab tree, but the sub-Sahelian sun had moved over his left shoulder so it was now beating down fiercely on the back of his head and he had been unable to move. The thorn bush under which he was hiding had been stripped almost bare and its skeletal shadow offered little shade.

He had been warned to be silent, absolutely silent. He listened for sounds. It was very quiet. A whisper of wind moved the dry grasses and was gone. He could hear himself breathing. He tried to calm it and breathe more slowly, more quietly. High above a vulture circled and looked down. He could not hear it. He looked to his right. He was sure his neck creaked. *Only thirty three*, he thought, *and I can hear my neck joints. It's early arthritis.*

Momadou was still by his side, unmoving in the full sun, a slight sheen of sweat on his forehead, but no signs of discomfort. David reached out slowly to touch his left elbow. At first there was no response but after some seconds he saw a frown on the African's forehead and the subtlest shaking of his head. They continued to wait in the afternoon heat. David's tongue was dry, his lips cracking. A bead of sweat rolled down the outside of his nose. It stopped, itching intensely, but he dare not scratch it. After an eternity it was joined by another and the larger globule of fluid ran down over his burning salty skin, still sore from shaving that morning, and it stung as it entered a crack on his lip. He stayed still. Silent.

I shouldn't have come, he thought, *shouldn't have agreed to this.* The two of them had met three weeks previously when Momadou had brought his son to the village clinic. They were a fine looking pair. Momadou was taller than many of the local men. He had a proud face adorned with tribal markings, a broad, well muscled chest and had walked in with a confident bearing. His son too was well grown with no signs of the malnutrition seen in so many boys his age. Kebbah, David's interpreter in the clinic, had greeted the stranger respectfully and introduced him as the village hunter and a champion wrestler. His son had cut his leg. While David made some notes he had queried the need for a hunter in the village, as the only wild animals were the boars and the Muslim villagers didn't eat them.

'Exactly,' said Kebbah, 'Only white men like you eat them. So the pigs increase in number and eat the groundnuts that are an important crop for the villagers here. Momadou kills the pigs to protect the crops. He's a very good hunter.'

The conversation lapsed while David washed Lamin's dirty leg, cleaned a lengthy jagged cut and stitched it up. He gave him an anti-Tetanus injection. The boy's eyes watered but he did not flinch. His father nodded approvingly and then turned to Kebbah.

'He asks if you would like a pig to eat. He says there are a few left that still need to be killed.'

David had only been in Africa for three months and

was keen for new experiences. Seeing an opportunity, he accepted but also asked if he could go hunting with Momadou. As Kebbah interpreted, Momadou's face momentarily lost its composure and David lost track of the conversation between the two Africans. Eventually Kebbah had glanced up as though gauging a delicate situation and said, 'He will come for you after your clinic one day. It's best to hunt them in late afternoon.' and again the two Africans had conferred before Kebbah turned again and said, 'So now, doctor, we go on with the clinic.' Momadou had shaken hands all round and he and his son had left.

And that, thought David, *might have been that.* He had almost forgotten about it, so busy was his job, but suddenly, today, Momadou had come back. Not very convenient. Perhaps Momadou had even hoped he would not be able to come. But he had dropped everything and together they had set off into the bush.

From the direction of the sun David thought they were south of the village and perhaps two miles out near the groundnut farms. Momadou seemed to know exactly where they were, for the moment they arrived at this spot he'd indicated where David should sit and took up position next to him.

Now his knees were troubling him. He'd got into a squatting position like the Africans, but his knees were sore. Hell, they were really sore. He remembered how they had hurt coming down Helvellyn a year ago and being told about about wear and tear on the back of the kneecaps. All this suffering in silence... and come to think of it, his back was ... Wait! Momadou was on the move. He was creeping forward, still squatting, still silent, but why? Was there something out there? David looked out into the glare of the scrub, scanning from left to right and back again. Nothing. Momadou was still, but poised with his bow and arrow in hand and his machete slung over his back. David checked again. Just the slightest whispers of wind. He looked down. A yard in front of him a dung beetle struggled like Sisyphus up a sand slope with its precious ball of excrement. David imagined he could hear the grains of sand tumble past the beetle as it rolled its ball along. He watched, fascinated. When he looked up, Momadou was further away. How had he done that without being heard?

After some minutes Momadou was ten yards away from David, who had still not heard or seen anything new. David began to stand. Immediately, without looking back, Momadou swept his left arm out to indicate David should stop. There was anger, ferocity in the movement that brooked no argument; David stilled himself in a half-crouched posture. His knees burned. He waited. Then he heard. A whimper. A soft maternal grunt. Scratching. Over to his right. By the edge of the palm trees, where the ground might be moist. Momadou was moving again, preparing his bow. A squeal, another. Grunts. There was a family. He straightened himself to see better, but the thorn bushes and the dry grasses blocked his view. Stretching his knees, he set off in Momadou's footsteps.

Crack.

It wasn't loud. The twig was only millimeters across. The sound lasted milliseconds. Then a silence of milliseconds before the pigs squealed, grunted, roared and ran. David stood frightened at how fast they ran with their snouts down and legs stretched out. They raced through the scrub back into the denser cover of the palm trees and were gone in seconds. He stood with his arms raised in shock and fear of the pigs and then of Momadou who rose slowly and swore at him, shaking his head in disgust.

In the fading light of evening the walk home was a silent and uncomfortable one. When they came within sight of the village, Momadou pointed the way and stood back, refusing to go further with David.

Three weeks later Momadou reappeared in the middle of a clinic, saying he had a fresh dead pig if David still wanted it. David rose to shake the hunter by the hand and apologize for his clumsiness in the bush. Momadou nodded his eyes steady on David, but talking to Kebbah.

'He says you were lucky. The pigs often attack if they have their babies with them. It is over now. He says you should look after the children, and he will kill the pigs. That way you are equally skilled, but neither of you knows the other man's work.'

That's really put me in my place, thought David, *down with the craftsmen and traders.*

After the clinic David went home for lunch, only to be greeted by his bemused and angry wife standing by the dead pig on their patio. For a moment the two of them stared at each other before laughing at their latest challenge. Four tiring hours later the skin was off, the pig was butchered, and something resembling chops, pork belly and other cuts of meat had been produced. That evening for the first time they enjoyed the fine gamey flavour of wild African boar, tough though it was to chew.

David stayed two more years in the village. During that time Momadou or his wife occasionally brought their children to see him. They were rich enough to buy food for their family and feed them throughout the year. Several pigs arrived on David's doorstep. Momadou always refused payment, simply saying that the doctor looked after the children. In the end, David didn't really feel put down by this, indeed, he began to feel quite pleased. He had a place in the village. He was acknowledged by the villagers as the doctor, as the man who looked after their children. He had a status.

Towards the end of the second rainy season David realized that he had not seen Momadou for some time, nor had any pigs been delivered to their house even though the groundnuts were growing in the fields. One day after the clinic, he stepped out into the now familiar wall of heat and humidity. How warm the sun, how bright the bougainvilleas, the flame trees! He turned back to Kebbah.

'Where's Momadou? I haven't seen him for a long time.'

'He's moved south to another region.'

'Why? He belonged to this village.'

'True, but there are no pigs left here now. His work is done and he had to move on.'

'What, no pigs! Why not?'

'Like I said, he was a good hunter. And you ate almost the last one. That's why you had so few recently.'

'So few. I didn't realize. Oh my God!'

'Yes, the groundnuts are undisturbed now. The farmers are happy.'

It was three days before David had time to go out

to where he and Momadou had waited so long in silence. This time he took the Land Rover and went alone. Opening the door, he climbed onto the vehicle's roof and looked round the deserted scrubland. Was the Sahara really closer than before? Certainly more trees had been cut down for firewood. David sat again in the sun watching the world around him. Not a breath of wind. Occasional weavers flew to and fro from their nests. No other sounds.

And then he heard it. The absence of the pigs. In his mind, a squeal, a grunt, but in the real world, just silence. They had gone. He listened again. Silence. He was a predator at the top of the food chain and he had killed his prey. Now, the silence was his to digest. '*Now,*' he told himself uncomfortably, '*now I really know my place.*'

Sister Francis

Maidy Clark

Sister Francis walked between the rows of desks, her suede shoes silent on the floor. She thumped a ruler into the palm of her left hand. The children sat erect, staring forward as she peered down at their open books inspecting the homework. Her head nodded with approval for most of them. She looked up and around the room, looking over the green jumpers, dark hair and olive skins. Her glance came to a halt as always as they reached the blond hair. Pausing at the child's desk she peered down. A warm glow settled in the pit of her stomach.

'Well, well, well, and what particular excuse do you have for this shameful piece of work?' Holding the book high between forefinger and thumb she exhibited it to the rest of the class. The other children obligingly giggled. 'Did you hear me? What's your excuse today?' She noticed the child put her hand to her stomach.

'I'm sorry Sister Francis, but a friend of my mother's spilt her cocktail on my book. It was late last night, and I didn't have…..'

Sister Francis held up her hand and silence reigned the room.

'Stand on your chair.'

The girl raised her face to her, and she could see the confusion in her eyes. The warmth spread upwards. She ran her tongue over her teeth enjoying the smooth sensation and sweet taste in her mouth.

'I said, stand on your chair. You're English aren't

you? Or don't you understand your own language?'

The classroom erupted with laughter.

'Now let's see, it's the fifth time in two weeks you've had trouble with your homework.'

The child stared ahead. The warm glow turned to a knot in Sister Francis' stomach, her throat grew hot, she knew her voice was going to rise and cleared her throat trying to control it. To make the speech effective, she knew from past experience she needed to start quietly.

'No homework last Tuesday, because you were at the Governor's Palace celebrating the Queen's Birthday. Only half done on Wednesday because your parents held a party, and you claimed you didn't have time to do it. Ah you did manage your weekend homework I notice. Let's give Miss Josephine a clap class, shall we.' She brought her hands together in a slow rhythmic movement. 'But then of course you fell asleep in class Monday. The excuse, had too much to drink, and kept you awake all night. You certainly do have a very creative imagination.' She paused for breath, and took a look around the room. She felt eyes on her, appreciating her skill as the girl's shoulders sagged. Moving her face next to the child's ear increasing the volume she continued.

'How dare you make up stories about your parents.' She enjoyed watching the child shake, the glow starting to replace the knot once more. 'At eleven years old you're old enough to be responsible. I hope you prayed for forgiveness, for you'll surely need it. You'll be going to Hell my child.' Sister Francis remembered the ruler in her hand, and for a split second she imagined it making contact with that white soft skin. The picture in her mind released more of the anger and her mouth watered, as she let her tongue run over her smooth teeth once more. She swallowed. Then slammed the ruler hard on the desk, feeling orgasmic joy as the child jumped.

'Now turn round!' she ordered.

With Josephine's back to her, she felt in her pocket for the two large safety pins, then very carefully, so as not too hurt the child in any way she pinned the offending book to her back. A few gasps from the other children were just audible, and Sister Francis let her lips curl in what she thought was a smile.

'Line up for Mass.' She watched as the other children moved slightly away from Josephine, and the child put her hand to her stomach, gently rubbing, her eyes concentrating on some distant object.

'Pray hard that Jesus forgives you,' she told the blond head as the whole class walked across the courtyard to the chapel to meet the rest of the school for morning mass.

***

The next morning as she looked around the classroom she noticed the child slipping something into her desk.

'What're you doing, Josephine?'

The child looked up at her, and Sister Francis noticed she was even paler than normal. Her blue eyes larger, looking at her in fear.

'Nothing Sister Francis.'

'You're lying! You'll go to Hell. Now tell me what you were doing.' She watched as the child's shoulders sank and her eyes died. Sister Francis smiled to herself as she walked to the desk.

'Open it up!' She lifted the desk, and Sister Francis noticed an envelope, addressed to her.

'What's this?' Silence. She looked into the desk again, and pushed some of the books aside. There were more envelopes, all with her name on them. 'What're all these doing here? Go and stand in the corridor, and if Mother Superior comes along you tell her how bad you've been. Go on get out. You evil child.'

She walked back to her desk, taking the envelopes with her.

'Class, turn to page 39 and proceed with exercise 2. In silence.'

Opening them one by one, she discovered they were all written by the girl's mother. They explained the difficulties she may have with her homework. The invitation to the Governor's Palace, the parties she had to attend, flying to Tangier for the weekend or Madrid for the day, she really didn't have time for all this homework and could Sister Francis please stop asking her to do it. She had to read them again.

The bell broke her thoughts of this awful woman who called herself a mother. Somewhere deep inside she felt a spark of compassion for the child.

The child, she must still be in the corridor!

'Juan, go and tell her to come back in now, please. The rest of you hand in your books, then go outside.'

'Sister Francis, she's not there,' Juan told her.

The compassion died. How dare that child defy her. Putting the letters in her drawer she marched off to look for her.

Opening the door of the girls' toilet, she called.

'Are you in there, child?' Silence. She began to check the cubicles, pushing each one open. As she pushed the door of the last one her hand flew to her mouth.

The girl hung by her tie from the hot pipe, her feet swaying very gently from the movement of the door. Sister Francis put her hand to her stomach and rubbed.

The River

Peter Smerdon

I have always been drawn to water. I didn't like swimming in the stuff, I just spluttered along and slowly sank to the bottom. Never could see the point of swimming. But on or beside the water, that was something different. To me, that was life, always different, always something to be seen. Hardly surprising really, considering my background. My grandfather, his father, his father…oh, I don't exactly know how far back, had all been pilots on the River. You had to be a member of one of five families just to be considered for the job. You should have seen the pilot boats in those days. Fast, seaworthy launches, beautifully maintained. Their dark blue hulls contrasted with the varnished woodwork and the polished brass fittings. The engine room, with two powerful diesel engines, was kept clean enough to eat in. They were proper boats.

My great uncle, although he could not be a pilot as he had only married into the family, had been a foy boatman on the River. When I found out what this meant, I thought he must be one of the bravest (or maybe stupidest) men I knew. He used to row around in a small wooden boat, taking the cables from the great ships that wanted to moor in the basin and passing them through the rings on the mooring buoys and then back to the ship's crew. These weren't bits of rope like the clothesline in your back garden – they were as thick as a strong man's thigh and heavy enough to swamp or upset a boat like his. Foy boatmen didn't normally retire – they just conveniently drowned when their strength slipped away. So, I reckoned that the River ran through my veins.

I was very unhappy to discover as a youngster that because there were hardly any ships coming into the river, I couldn't make a living as a pilot. No one wanted the "black gold" any more; it was too dirty and inconvenient. Why shovel out ash from a coal fire if you could just flick a switch or turn a tap? So, the mines closed and the bulk carriers stopped coming into the river. Bang went the livelihood of many of the people on the River, including the pilots.

Nevertheless, I was determined to make my living on the River. To me, it was something alive. How something that started as a few drops of water miles away in the hills of the north could turn into a powerful ever-flowing serpent, that gave work and food to many, but could also snatch away a careless life, always fascinated me.

I was a bit of a likely lad. At school, my mates always told me I was gobby and I was ever the first to try all the vices that came our way. Although, I think in truth we were fairly innocent then – it was just drink, tobacco and a bit of a fumble with the girls. Kids nowadays seem to have many more options available to destroy their souls.

When I left school, my father lent me a bit of money and I bought a clapped-out motor boat. I gave her what I thought was a belter of a paint job – a black hull with a broad red stripe on the waterline and sparkling white upper works. I spent my small savings on a bigger outboard, renamed her *Addiction* and I was in business. I took punters out for fishing and diving trips and quickly learnt the best places for the fish and where the most interesting wrecks were. As a result, business prospered and with each increase in fortune, I bought a slightly larger boat with more powerful engines. By the time of *Addiction IV*, I had a craft that would cope with anything the British weather could deliver.

One night in the pub, I was taken aside by someone I had seen around and who I knew to be a bit of a villain. He bought me a drink, we had a quiet chat and I found myself with a new line of work, doing night runs to the continent to collect "goods". I didn't inquire closely what the goods were and they didn't tell me. The money rolled in, my mates in the river police tipped me the wink as to when I should come and go and I made sure they could afford the little luxuries of life.

I had a nice flat on the waterside, a sports car in the garage and a succession of beautiful, but expensive, girlfriends. I loved women – and they loved to help me out with my lifestyle. I made sure that I changed them on a regular basis as I didn't want anything too permanent. I wasn't being hard hearted, just objective. I wanted my business to remain my business – and only mine. So, as soon as a girl started to hint that wouldn't it be better if she moved in with me, wouldn't it be cosy? – that was when I looked around for someone new.

By now, human traffic had become the most profitable cargo. I only dealt with the upper end of the market, where the potential earning power of the girls in question meant that they had to be treated very carefully and not just dumped into a container like some poor sods we read about in the papers. I carried no more than six at any time, in relative comfort as long as the sea wasn't too rough. If the forecast was poor, I fed them anti seasickness tablets and bedded them down with a bucket apiece. At cruising speed, I could do the trip in fifteen hours. The girls had minimal English language skills but their other personal attributes outweighed what might under normal circumstances be seen as a prerequisite for employment in England. I made a trip every month or so and in the meantime, continued with the fishing and diving trips, to account for my now lavish lifestyle.

I guess you could describe my moral compass as being rather elastic. I didn't set out to be this way and I tried not to damage anyone, but as time went on, I began to have more qualms about the life that I was transporting these girls too. If I had had more sense, looking back, I should have found another line of work at this point. But I didn't, arguing with myself that after a few more trips, I could get out of this life completely and buy myself a proper business. What is it they say about the road to hell? Hindsight is a wonderful thing.

Just after Christmas, I was asked to make another trip. I looked at the weather outlook and got a very bad feeling – a succession of vigorous lows was forecast to cross the country. I tried to get the trip postponed but my contact told me that the girls had already been waiting for five days and if I didn't want the job, they would get someone else. Like it or lump it, was the message. I looked at the forecast again and decided I could get across once the current low pressure had blown through, sit over there for twelve hours whilst the succeeding system did its worst, then return. My contact said this was acceptable. So, as darkness fell, I slipped the warps off the quayside and headed out to sea.

The wheelhouse was lit only by the instrument lights; forward, I could see the faint red and green glow of the navigation lights, tossing from side to side as the swell moved the vessel around. As we left the River, I moved the throttle levers down, the engine noise ramped up and the boat speed increased. I set the autopilot and poured myself a cup of coffee from the thermos by the helmsman's chair. I had a long night ahead.

I arrived at my destination as dawn was breaking. I moored the boat up, went ashore, met my contact and the girls were led aboard. I told them that they should rest whilst I slept and that we would be leaving that evening. Normally, I struggled to make myself understood, but this time, one very pretty brunette told me she understood me and relayed my instructions to the others. I led them below, showed them their bunks, the toilet and kitchen facilities and left them to it. I had always made it clear to my contacts that I was the bus driver, not the tour guide.

I was conscious that whilst I slept fitfully, the wind increased – the movement of the boat to its warps and the sound of the wind and water against the hull told me this. When I got up at 14.00, I looked out. Clouds were scudding across the sky, but it did look as though the front had blown through as predicted. I listened to the weather forecast and this promised that wind speeds would decrease. So, I told the girls that we would be leaving in an hour and if they wanted something to eat, now would be a good time, and that they should take the tablets I laid out for them. Again, the pretty brunette translated for me. I made myself sandwiches and coffee, ate and drank some immediately and put the rest in the wheelhouse for the long night ahead. At 16.00 we departed. The brunette joined me in the wheelhouse.

'Do you mind if I stay with you for a while?' she asked.

'I don't mind, but you might feel better if you were lying down. It might get a bit lumpy out there.'

'Lumpy?' she queried.

'Oh, sorry; the sea might be a bit rough.'

'Ah,' she said with a grin. 'I like that, yes, lumpy,' storing away this English idiom. She added, 'I went out on boats with my father. He was a fisherman. So, I don't get seasick.'

'That's helpful,' I said. 'Your English is very good. Where did you learn it?'

'My father sold his fish to an Englishman who lived in our village. I think he liked me, so he taught me your language. That is, until my father drowned. So, now I have to go to work in your country to help support my mother and brothers and sisters.'

I just grunted at that. There wasn't much else I could say. As we made progress back to England, we got to know each other better. Karin wanted to know about where she was going. I tried to help as much as I could, but all the time I was trying to avoid saying too much about what she would be doing once she got there. I was never clear how much the girls knew; my rubber band conscience hoped that they knew exactly but my realistic self kept telling me that was unlikely.

I liked her. I liked her a lot. And of course, I felt sorry for her. She was clearly an intelligent, amusing and attractive woman put into horrible circumstances by the unfortunate death of her father.

However, once we were past the point of no return on the journey, I began to be more worried about the safety of us all. The wind had gradually been increasing and the sea state getting rougher. I was now seeing gusts of over 30 knots on the wind speed indicator. I had to throttle back the engines and the boat was rolling and pitching violently. From below, I could hear the sounds of retching. I told Karin to strap herself into the other chair in the wheelhouse and I tied myself into the helmsman's chair. We kept going, albeit much more slowly. Karin stayed awake with me all night, feeding me coffee and sandwiches as necessary, and keeping me entertained with tales of her family. Gradually, the distance to our destination reduced and I began to relax.

As a result of the weather, our journey had been much slower than planned. The second front had blown through, conditions were improving and I thought all our troubles were behind us when a fast-moving blip appeared on my radar, heading for us. From its speed, I thought it was probably the coastguard cutter. I opened the throttles as much as I could and hoped that I could outrun her. The boat plunged through the swells, the powerful outboards screaming as the propellers lifted out of the water.

'What are we doing,' asked Karin in alarm. 'Are we in trouble?'

'We might be.'

I was concentrating on my radar screen, trying to

work out whether I could outrun our pursuer. I thought so – the distance between us was now increasing. Suddenly, the wheelhouse was full of noise.

'What the bloody hell….?'

I looked around. Karin had slipped out of her chair and opened the wheelhouse door onto the open cockpit aft, to be able to see better. She stood for a moment at the door, then slipped into the cockpit and across to the side guardrails.

'Karin, come back, it's not safe out…'

As I shouted the warning, I lost concentration, and *Addiction* turned sharply to starboard. Karin was thrown off balance, teetered for a moment on top of the guardrails, her feet scrabbling desperately for grip, then she disappeared over into the sea.

'Oh, hell.' Caught between the devil and the deep blue sea. Various options ran through my mind. Stay or flee? No, despite my dodgy moral compass, there was really only one choice. I pressed the man overboard button on my chart plotter, marking the position where she went into the sea, turned the wheel over and picked up my radio-telephone to make a mayday call.

Karin comes to see me every week in my current abode, living at Her Majesty's pleasure. I reckon, with time off for good behaviour, I should be out in another eighteen months. Every time she comes, we talk about the future, rather than the past. She blames herself for my predicament but actually, what happened to her forced me to change my lifestyle. Fortunately, I found her before she had been in the water too long. At that time of year, it's reckoned that an individual in the water will be dead within fifteen minutes.

I plan to go back to work on the River, but this time I'll stick to fishermen and divers. I bought Karin out of her contract and she's living in my flat, looking after the place. When I get out, we'll take things slowly, but I have hopes that we might have a future together. I can't see the River from the window of my cell, but I sometimes think that in the dead of a misty night, I can hear the foghorn blowing. I know it's out there still.

His Bag for Life

Penny McCulloch

The plastic carrier bag for life
lay flat
in the hallway,
unpacked.
In it was a pair of deep
red pyjamas, face cloth
and false teeth
shower gel and underpants,
leaflets
about stomach cancer
and recovery from keyhole surgery,
my sorrow
about the easily digestible
meals I did not
get to cook for him,
a mobile phone - very useful
as a family telephone directory,
a small transistor tuned to radio four
a torn copy of The Guardian
a puzzlebook, notepad and pen
his wisdom's passing

the get well card

from his brother,

the book of cricket quotes

I never gave him,

the empty space

in my heart,

the swell

of my unshed tears.

Dating with animals

Derek Miller

Arriving just in time is generally my style, but this time I was a little late as the room was round the back and up the stairs. When asking directions from the barman he did give me a look to say "total loser" before directing me in the right direction.

The room was up some wooden stairs and along a corridor with some awful colour tiles and a yellow stained ceiling. Opening a creaking door, which had the sign "Speed Dating in Style" I went in and was not surprised to be indicated towards the bar and then a seat in the corner. As soon as I sat down the organiser said that for today as a change the men sit still and the women move round, with a slot of five minutes with each person. With ten people this means I have to appear to be reasonable for about an hour.

Both my publisher and next door neighbour said that I should try speed dating. I'm pushing fifty and haven't had a partner for about ten years. I was sent an email about the next session for over forties at the Black Hound in Leamington. So on Thursday I had a shower, washed and combed my hair, put on my least faded jeans that weren't ripped, a decent not too worn blue shirt, slung on my parka and took the bus.

It was a room at the back of the pub, large enough for ten old misshapen wooden tables to be set out in a sort of decagon shape with grim, grey, padded chairs for the men on the outside. The decorations seemed dated and tired, the wallpaper was losing colour, worn off in a random fashion like an image of the moon surface. Looking round I did think I may stand a chance as some of the other men appeared in an even worse state than me. So I was confidently sipping my pint, taking it easy there's plenty of time to drink afterwards, and certainly not at these prices. I eased down into the chair and expected to be viewed like an exhibit in a museum.

The women were chatting to each other, mainly in groups of two or three and had probably just come out for a bit of fun, although one or two looked a little more desperate.

On the way there I did work out ways to sound impressive and knowledgeable about the books I'd written called "Procrastination for Clever People" and "Keep your Clutter". I was the named author although they had been written mainly by copying from other people. The rest of my life is not that great and the writing just about pays the rent on the flat but doesn't leave enough to run a car. When I described myself on the application form as an author it was perhaps just a little bit of an embellishment.

Like a number of women there, the first one at my table had probably over eaten at some time in her life, couldn't shift the excess weight and I was concerned for the chair. She did shake hands and I was not quick enough to move away; afterwards I just wanted to use a wipe. Too much red lipstick is unbecoming on a woman, and any more than one earring makes a face look lopsided. Even though she annoyed me, I tried not to breathe on her, because earlier on in the day I'd forgotten I was going out so I had started drinking cider in my flat.

One of her questions was; 'What about the sexual

references in George Elliot, do you think it shows repression?'

I replied 'I've no idea, I write technical books and have never read anything written by him.'

She seemed to lose interest after that and was glad when the bell rang to move on.

It was a numbers game, with probably less chance than winning the lottery. The next woman, perhaps not quite as large as the first, asked about my views on asylum seekers, and then declared me an ignorant fascist when I mentioned about sending them back.

The third woman just sat down and started to talk. I knew there was a chance when she approached, she was the right size. She had blond hair down to middle of shoulders with high heels, black jacket and pencil skirt with a white blouse and a red flower brooch. With an attractive face, lines on her brow were almost concealed with make-up, and her pretty mouth was just a little lopsided. She had been through a few problems in her life I thought, and looked at little older than forty-five which was the age I guessed her to be.

'Hello, I'm Deidre, just as a starting question, do you like The Voice or X Factor or do you just watch the News?'

She was very measured in her speech but not over confident. I wondered what she was doing here, so out of place, but I wasn't supposed to ask that. It was a good opening question, quite friendly and focussed. So I tried to match her tone and hoped it wasn't too forced. 'Hello I'm Simon. I do like to keep up to date with what is going on, often by listening to the radio when I'm travelling or cooking, but then I do also like The Voice.'

She smiled at the answer and I was so pleased that I'd looked at the website for the best answers to questions on the way here. Her next question was also out of the book so perhaps she was more nervous than me. 'I like The Voice as well. What do you do for a living? I'm a lecturer in business studies at the college.'

'I'm an author and write books on technical subjects such as time management and minimalist living.' This was my stock answer designed to impress, and it did seem to work.

'That sounds very interesting and I'm sure we can talk more about books later.' I was hoping a lot later because I don't read any books. She continued, 'What would you take with you to a desert island?'

I must have looked at the same web site so there was a pre-recorded answer in my head, only just a little different from the reality. 'It would have to be a few good books and a boules set. I've always wanted to play well; it seems such an engaging game when played in the square in French villages.' Well this is close to reality, and then I asked; 'Do you like outdoor activities?'

'I don't follow football, and I do love walking in the country.'
I just had time to say; 'So do I, it's so good to be outdoors' before the bell rang for her to move on.

The rest of the night was more of a blur, and I lost interest.

Deidre and I must have ticked the same boxes because amazingly enough we both agreed by text to meet again, and as the weather was set to be reasonable she suggested a day at the zoo, and I was happy with that suggestion. The day started well, at least the alarm went off and I had time for a shower. Being just a few minutes late, due to the bus taking longer than expected, was very good for me. I was dressed in my usual tee shirt, jeans, red jumper, a warm blue parka and old boots. Arriving at her house I was looking forward to today. Deidre had dressed for a fashion show. Very flat open-toed sandal, short skirt, she did have good legs, and strapless top with a cardigan the same colour as limes. I had to look away. People should just not wear green. It is associated with a feeling of restless energy and bad luck.

Her light coloured, small car was comfortable enough, she was a quick driver and we were soon there. She had probably looked at the weather forecast because as soon as I got there it was so hot I regretted putting on my parka and had to carry it round.

The day started to go downhill from then. I offered to buy the coffees as she had driven us here; I made the usual excuses about my car in for a service which is true except that it's been in the garage for three years. But as I was carrying the tray some little kid ran towards me and I jerked out of the way spilling most of the drinks. By the time I thought to say something the toddler was out of sight.

Then at the first enclosure, with a glass front there were two cute looking monkeys. This idyllic scene soon turned to anguish as one of the monkeys started playing with himself, which was quite funny to start with, but then when his partner joined in and then started having sex on the bench in front of the window I thought it was time to move on. Deidre was quite a good sport at this point, but we were both keen to leave this scene.

'Let's look at the leopards' I suggested.

But the leopards were nowhere to be seen and I wanted to keep going. Deidre was a slow walker and wanted to look everywhere, even when there was nothing to be seen. The gorillas were baring their backsides and urinating in front of us. I don't want to see this at the best of time, and certainly not when I'm trying to impress someone. The elephants were so grey and boring and just move slowly, this zoo is not as interesting as I remember.

She started talking about whether or not the animals were happy. 'Those giraffes look so forlorn and lonely licking the posts and trying to get some nourishment out of those branches.'

I wasn't that bothered; 'They're here for our benefit and should be grateful for food and water.'

'That's quite a narrow way of looking at this issue. Don't you think animals have some rights, and should live a more peaceful existence in the wild?' She was looking at me intensely.

'We pay to come in.' Not that I was concerned, it was expensive enough to get in anyway.

Stopping for a sit down and looking at the scene in front of us with flowering cherries producing masses of pink blossoms on bare branches. All I can really say is; 'It's very nice here.'

'Springtime is fantastic, the scent of the newly cut box hedges produce a wonderful smell. As the wind blows the clouds move to show the sun then petals fall down from the tree.' She moves her hand towards mine, as I leant forward to take off my shoes and shake out a stone. I do wish I'd worn more sensible footwear and socks without holes.

We walk on; I do like to be slightly apart, avoids the risk of accidental or deliberate contact.

At lunchtime my knowledge of the cuisine impressed her I think. I choose foods that don't take too much away from the taste of brown sauce, so generally go for the English option of something and chips. She went for some foreign stuff that looked lively for me. Conversation was a bit stilted; she knew so much stuff about which I'd never heard, well who wants to know about these foreign countries.

She asked about my working day, 'Do you spend most of your time writing?'

'Well no, most of the day is spent watching TV, playing computer games and sitting in the garden.' She started playing with her sunglasses. 'Writing my books does not take up much time at all. Basically I cut and paste from other blogs on the web, change a little bit, think of a snappy title then send it to my publisher. My last effort, "Focus for Success" was completed in about four weeks, there's so much material available. I don't like spending too much time on them. And the income keeps me in cider.'

'Is that all you do, drink and watch the television?' She was starting to look a little puzzled at this point.

'Yes, what else is there?' I was realising that this was almost my limit for being reasonable.

'Presumably then you don't have any friends, why did you go speed dating?' The lines around her mouth were more prominent now.

'Well I thought it would be good to try as I don't have many friends.'

'Why did you pick me, out of all the girls there?'

I was picking my way through the chips and sauce; 'I'm not sure, you were the only one who was not too fat, some of the others were huge.'

'I can't see why I ticked any of the boxes for you,' Deidre said in a quite definitive way as she got up.

I was glad in a way that it ended quite quickly when I realized how much it cost to go out for the day, and I hadn't brought that much money out with me.

She left with a wave and said; 'Well goodbye, maybe I'll see you around.' She left me to find my own way home on the bus. I always knew it would end in tears when she wore that colour.

Trish and Chips

Paul Chiswick

Jean-Paul, every night I dream of you as you gaze at the lazy glide of the Seine, the city lights bright in your dark eyes, your strong hands . . .
Delete, delete, delete.

Trish shook her head. Had she taken leave of her senses? Girls of fifteen behaved like this, mooning over some boy band member. She told herself to act her age, behave like a mature woman of thirty-six should. Then, for what seemed like the hundredth time, she stared at Jean-Paul's photo in the Skype window, placed her finger on it and felt her heart judder.

Oh God, he's gorgeous, she thought.

She had circumnavigated chat rooms (there might be some pervert or twelve-year-old on the line); fiddled with Facebook (too public, who wants the world to know your business?); dallied on dating sites (promising, but pay those fees? No way). No, Skype suited her purpose just fine. She could text or talk, be visible or hidden: her choice. She had taken things slowly, built her relationship with Jean-Paul one step at a time using the message line. When the time was right and she wanted to see and hear him, all she had to do was turn on the webcam.

Her fingers hovered over the keyboard.
Is it raining in Paris?
No. Here is a perfect evening. It rains in Manchester?
It always rains in Manchester.

You watch French swimming team? Very good, yes?

Sorry, I work in the evening.

Why had she shown a complete disinterest in the Olympics? Recently, his written questions had come thick and fast. *You watch opening ceremony? No, I had some shopping to do. You think Phillips Idowu turn up? I'm sure he will.* (Phillips Idowu?) *English footballers, they have chance? I think they will make the quarter final.* (Her brother, Dale, a Manchester City fan had expressed this opinion only recently.) *What formation you think team have? 4-4-2? I think so, maybe.* (Formation?)

You work in evening? What you do?

Her fingers froze. If she told him the truth he would be out of her life faster than Usain Bolt ran a hundred metres. (Amazingly, she did know who he was. Then again, who didn't?)

I'm an auxiliary.

Auxiliary?

I work in a hospital, helping nurses.

Ah, I understand.

Where are you? Are you close to the river?

Ah, oui, I am in little café called Les Marguerites. I think this mean The Daisies in English. Very pretty. Very, how you say, romantic?

Her skin tingled. She conjured up a picture of the café edging the Seine: paintings by local artists on pastel walls; a barman in a blue beret polishing gleaming wine glasses; perfumed fragrance of flowers mingling with the aroma of garlic and onions drifting in from the kitchen. Jean-Paul and she sat opposite each other, his warm hands stroking hers, his sibilant French (she wouldn't understand more than a sprinkling of words, but what did that matter?) sending butterflies fluttering in her stomach. At some point, on some unseen signal, they would rise, glide towards each other. She would melt in the pools of his eyes, almost faint with the ecstasy of it. His lips, full, moist, would seek out hers.

She sighed, whispered, 'Oh, Jean-Paul,' and reached for the webcam.

'Mum, Dad's on the phone. He wants to talk to you.'

Her stomach lurched. She spun round just as her sixteen-year-old son, Ciaran, leaned over her shoulder.

'Who's Jean-Paul?'

'He . . . he's someone I know at work.'

'But he's.... '

'Ciaran, would you mind? This is private.'

Patricia, the evening it is perfect for lovers. Stars, moon, a cool breeze. You feel it also?

Ciaran's eyes narrowed.' What are you up to, Mum?'

'Ciaran!'

'Okay, okay.'

'Well? What are you waiting for?'

'Like, Dad's on the phone.'

'Tell him I'll be there in a second.'

'Shall I say you're Skypeing Jean-Paul?'

'Ciaran . . .'

My friend is on the phone, Jean-Paul. Can you wait five minutes?

Bien sûr.

'Jimmy. What can I do for you?'

'Something's come up at work, Trish. I'm going to be late home.'

'Again?'

'Give me a break. I'm doing this for us.'

She cursed him under her breath. Like hell he was. Over the years she had listened to his excuses with strained patience. She had always wondered why Jimmy's secretaries changed on a regular basis. Wondered, that is, until one of them, a girl hardly out of school, had phoned and plunged a knife deep into his back. For Ciaran's sake Trish had bottled up her anger, clamped her mouth and prayed the girl would be the last of Jimmy's infidelities. Some hope. Now, as Ciaran teetered on the edge of manhood, payback time had come.

'Okay. I'll wrap up something for you when I'm finished at the chip shop.'

She took a deep breath, flexed her fingers and began to compose the message.

Does your laptop have a camera?
Of course.
Is it switched on?
Moment. Yes, is on now. Also the mike.

She straightened her back, patted her hair with her hand, turned on the webcam. Jean Paul's face popped up in the Skype window. His eyes were as in his picture, but the glistening, hairless head was a surprise. And, instead of the clean-cut jaw, a scruffy beard the colour of cigarette ash covered most of his lined face.

Trish felt as if a stake had been driven through her

heart.

A flicker of a smile lingered on Jean-Paul's lips then faded. She knew in an instant the reason. Her photo had been taken years ago, before habitual snacking on the chip shop's leftovers bloated her.

The video window blanked.

For what seemed like an eternity she stared at the screen. Then the Skype message line came to life.

You watch Usain Bolt? Incredible, non?

Friends Reunited

Maidy Clark

Looking through his office door, he saw everyone busy concentrating on their own monitors. Moving the mouse around the mat, he clicked on the icon for his own private email. The symbol showed he had six messages. Scanning then, he sucked in his breath. There it was, her name. It had worked. She had sent him a message. Fumbling with the mouse, ignoring the others he clicked on her name.

>*Subj: Contact from Friends Reunited – Fiona Cox*
>*Date: 22/6/2002 15:47:27 GMT Daylight Time*
>*From: Funismine@aol.com*
>*To: Andysmith@BT.co.uk*
>*This is a message from Fiona Cox email:Funismine@aol.com who is contacting you through http://www.friendsreunited.co.uk*
>*The message is as follows:-*
>*Hey Andy,*
>*I saw your name listed. What are you doing registering under an all girls school? Was such a shock to see you there. Let me know how you are. I am well. Working hard down here in Brighton. Making loads of money. I fell straight into this job after school. And have done really well here. It is a PR company, we manage some big contracts. Have to go, so busy. Write and tell me your news.*

Fi.

Andy read the message again and again. It had really worked. His hands shook as he started to type his reply. Then he deleted it all, walked away to get a coffee. Now he had to decide what to reply. How to reply? What should he tell her? All of it, or not? No, he would be cool, as the young kids said. Play it cool. He ran a damp hand through his hair, as he stared at the monitor reading it again. Then clicked on the print icon. He held it in his hands, folded it carefully, then slipped it in his pocket.

***

'Just going out for a cigarette,' he yelled slamming the back door.

He walked in the dark round to the garage, lighting his cigarette as he went. Flicking the switch of the garage light, he blinked to accustom his eyes to the light. He pulled out the brick and felt inside with his hand, his heart beating as it did every time. Catherine went through everything so thoroughly he had had to think and work carefully on this hiding place. She would never find this one.

Holding the book gently he opened it to see her face smiling up at him. As beautiful and clear as the day it was taken. Laminating it had been a good idea. He sighed. Turning the pages there were others, mixed in with the letters and reports. Taking out the morning's email, he smoothed out the creases and added it to the book. There were still a few empty pages, but now he knew these would soon be full.

Stamping on the butt, he gave a final look around

then flicked the switch back off, shutting the door.

**

He put his coffee down on the desk, then clicked on the icon to write a message.

> *Subj: Friends Reunited*
> *Date: 23/06/02 09:07:34 GMT Daylight Time*
> *From: Andysmith@BTNet.co.uk*
> *To: Funismine@aol.com*
> *Hi Fi,*
> *What a surprise to get your message. I hadn't realized that I had registered my name at the school. I thought I was just browsing. You sound well. I am married with one child. We live in a village called Storrington. It's very close to Brighton actually. Let me have all the news.*
> *Andy.*

He read it through. It had just the right tone, he was sure. Nothing too suggestive, leaving it wide open for her to make the first move. He clicked the mouse, and sighed heavily. All he had to do now was wait.

**

He put the windscreen wipers on fast. Squinting, his eyes trying to see, but lights blared into them coming from the other direction. Then he saw her. She stood in the doorway of her office, fighting with her umbrella. People rushed past. No one noticed her or him. He sat and watched. Then she made a dash for it. Water splashed her legs, soaking her fashionable shoes, but the umbrella protected her dark braided hair. Sitting back in the leather seat, he slipped the car into gear to follow her. She went straight home. He carried on driving, his wife would want to know why he was late, again.

***

Taking a drag on the cigarette he read the message again. Euphoria burst round his body at her suggestion they have lunch together. He had not expected this to happen so soon. His hand shook as he held it.

'Pull yourself together man,' he said out loud.

He smoothed the paper down, adding it to the rest of the messages. She had been rather prolific. He could sense the longing between them. If it hadn't been for those stuck up parents of hers, seeing him as low down and worth nothing, it would be Fi in the kitchen, not Catherine. Because he would never have slept with Catherine, and she would never have got pregnant. Now all that was going to change. He would write back tomorrow and they would have lunch next week. He must play it cool though. This must not be rushed, it must be done properly this time. He booked a table at The Grand, and then, just in case, booked a suite as well.

***

Looking at her across the table, he had to pinch himself. His imagination had taken him here so often. Feeling the condensation run down his fingers he raised his glass to her.

'Cheers Fi. It really is great to see you.' Smiling into her eyes they chinked their glasses.

'Cheers Andy. So tell me, what've you been up to?' She took a breath, then carried on. 'I really must tell you just quickly though, I've just landed this amazing contract. It should bring me thousands. They're all rather excited at the agency. I'm the blue eyed girl at the moment. Even if I say so myself, I am rather good.' Taking a breath, she forked some of the smoked salmon into her mouth, took a swig of Chardonnay then continued between mouthfuls.

His eyes followed her every move, the fork to her mouth, then the glass, her mouth opening and shutting while she whittled on and on. He moved his food around his plate with his fork while listening. She was really pleased with herself. Her eyes sparkled with enthusiasm. By the end of the meal, she had told him everything of her life and he had told her nothing. A cold splinter settled itself in his stomach.

'Do you have to rush off?' he asked, looking at his watch.

'Been to Tenerife I see.' She touched his gold Rolex with her painted fingernail. He smiled remembering how he had treated himself to the watch when he made his first million.

'Sorry?'

'Fake? It's fake right?'

'Oh,' he paused, then nodded his head, 'Yeah.'

'Well I must go.' She stood, her hand fell on his shoulder as she bent to kiss his cheek. 'Beautiful,' she said as she smoothed the silk of his Savile Row suit. 'It's amazing what you can get from these factory outlet shops, isn't it?'

'Well actually,....' he paused looking into her eyes. There was no point.

***

As the key goes in the lock, his wife starts.

'I've been so worried. Where've you....'
'Not another word!'

He sees her mouth close as she takes in the sight of him. Walking through the kitchen he catches a glimpse in the mirror of what she had seen: wind swept hair, grim face. Grabbing a beer from the fridge, he goes out of the French windows down the steps past the tennis court to the swimming pool. He sits in a deck chair thinking of her, and sees her face in front of him. The cold splinter grows.

***

In the garage he looks down at her photograph, tracing the lines of her face with his finger tips. Lighting his cigarette he draws heavily on it, then exhales as he walks to the corner where he keeps the jerry can. Flinging the completed book on the floor he soaks it in petrol, then draws heavily once more on his cigarette before throwing it on top of the book. He watches as the flames erupt immediately.

Lifting his head the flames reflect his face in the car window. Dull grey eyes stare back at him. A middle aged man, receding grey hair, furrows on his fore head. Realisation punches him hard in the stomach. He imagines his wife standing beside him. Her pretty round face, light mousy hair, kind brown eyes, smiling up at him. Andy stamps the flames out.

Walking through the French windows he sees Catherine in the kitchen, pinny on, cooking dinner. She looks up at him, worry stretched across her brow. He smiles and feels a warm glow settle inside, a feeling he has not felt for a long time. Sliding his arm around her waist he kisses her cheek.

A Poor Do

Elsa Halling

'Well, it's the right sort of weather for a funeral,' muttered Cousin Freda to her mother, Agnes. Flurries of winter rain battered the huddled figures gathered around the open grave in the bleak churchyard. The paltry group of mourners braced themselves against the biting wind which whipped against their clothes, threatening to make off with hats and turn umbrellas inside out. The daughter sprinkled a handful of sodden earth on the coffin. It made dull splodgy sound as it hit the oak lid of the casket that held the mortal remains of Sadie Wilson. Agnes prodded Freda sharply in the ribs.

'Your turn now, I can't be bendin' down, not in this weather. I'll never get up agen,' the old lady whispered.

'But I'll ruin me gloves, they're new ones, cost me twenty five quid in M&S.'

'Well, take 'em off then,' hissed her mother.

'But I'll get me hands filthy,'

'I've got some tissues in me pocket, never come to a funeral wi'out tissues.' She hadn't needed the tissues during the service. The relationship she had had with her older sister had never been close and Agnes had wasted neither tears nor tissues on Sadie's demise.

Finally the graveside ceremony was over and the group stepped cautiously between the granite headstones to make their way back to the gravel path and the shelter of the church porch.

'Where to next?' questioned Uncle George, as he pulled his scarf closer round his throat. It was already after midday and well past the time for his first pint.

'We've booked a buffet lunch at the Cat and Fiddle,' his niece, Marion told him

'But the Cat an' Fiddle's miles away, right up on t'moor.'

'Sorry Uncle George, but everywhere in the town was booked, impossible to find anywhere at short notice this time of year.' Marion gave her uncle a rueful smile. 'We've got enough transport for everyone, Ivy's kindly offered to take some of you and it won't take us above twenty minutes to get there.' Ivy and her companion, Alice, were two of her mother's childhood friends, the only non-family members of the party.

Marion and her husband, James shepherded the assembly into the cars and they headed off in a small convoy for the Cat and Fiddle.

High up on the moor the cars turned into the car park of the old stone inn. The sombrely clad figures emerged from the meagre cortege of vehicles and coalesced into a straggly group of crow-like figures flocking round road-kill.

'Let's get you all inside and into the warm.' Marion brightly ushered the mourners towards the inn door and into the function room. Food was already laid out and steaming urns of tea and coffee awaited them, but best of all was a huge log fire crackling in the ingle-nook. Warm rugs covered the stone floor and curtains depicting hunting scenes surrounded the leaded window panes.

'It were a bit short, weren't it?' Uncle Albert was

the first to speak.

'What, the service?'

'Aye.'

'Just as well, it were freezin' in't church and brass monkeys in that cemetery wi' wind blowin' off moors,' shivered Uncle George.

'Well what can you expect? The vicar didn't know 'er,' said Cousin Freda sharply. 'Why she 'ad to be brought all the way up 'ere I don't know. And who's going to look out for the grave now Iris has gone?'

Marion helped her cousin off with her coat, 'You know Mum always wanted to be buried alongside Dad; they bought a double plot, specially.' Marion defended her decision to have her mother's body brought back up to her Yorkshire birthplace from her home in the Midlands.

Freda and her mother headed for a wooden settle with bright red cushions which stood on one side of the inglenook and Ivy and Alice took possession of a small table on the opposite side.

'They've formed camps already,' whispered Marion to her husband James.

'Don't know why *'e* wanted to be brought up here in the first place,' put in Uncle Albert. ''E never came back much after they moved south. Thought we weren't good enough for 'im. Not wi' 'is posh degrees and bein' a headmaster an' all.' He gave 'headmaster' its aspirant to emphasise his scorn.

'He wasn't just a headmaster,' corrected Freda, 'he was a doctor.'

'Eeh, I didn't know that, why didn't he work in an 'ospital then?'

'Not a medical doctor Dad, he was a doctor of philosophy in mathematics.'

Uncle Albert shook his head, 'It's all beyond me.' He surveyed the room, assessing its suitability for the occasion, 'It's a bit bleak.'

'What did you expect, Dad, Christmas decorations? Wouldn't be exactly appropriate would it?' snapped Cousin Freda.

'Can't see any baked 'am,' muttered Uncle George as they found seats. 'Allus 'ave baked 'am at funerals,' he complained. 'Baked 'am, and a good rich fruit cake.'

'Now, who'd like tea?' Marion was anxious to change the subject. Baked ham and rich fruit cake were all very well for wakes at home or in a church hall, but no one had offered so she'd had to resort to the internet to find somewhere. Baked ham and rich fruit cake were not the style of this establishment. The elders of the party all opted for tea and she played waitress.

'What about you darling?' Marion turned towards James, her husband.

'I'll get some coffee,' he replied, more than happy to be an onlooker on the proceedings. It didn't do to get embroiled in discussions with his wife's northern relatives. They would be bound to gang up. 'A cup for you too?' Marion nodded her thanks.

'What's all these tandadlings?' Uncle George surveyed the spread. He poked at a plate of samosas. 'What's in them thur?'

'They're Indian, Uncle George, spicy, they're very good, try one.'

'Foreign muck.' Uncle George prodded a neatly

cut triangular sandwich. 'Huh, no crusts, best bit o't bread is crusts, nobbut a mouthful in these fiddly bits.' He took five of the smoked salmon dainties.

'What in heaven's name are tandadlings?' James whispered to his wife.

'Little cakes and pastries. Grandad always referred to fairy cakes and jam tarts as "tandadlings". He was another of the baked ham and fruit cake brigade,' Marion enlightened him, 'no idea where the word comes from though.'

'Why d'you think Uncle Donald wanted to come back up 'ere to be buried, Mam?' Cousin Freda had drawn the table close to the settle to ensure no one else could invade their space.

'I don't think they 'ad many friends down there; kept themselves to themselves.' She paused to take a bite of her samosa. 'These things aren't bad,' she remarked grudgingly. 'Anyway, 'e got really snooty and stuck up after that college education of his. I think he was a bit of a tartar too. I remember your Auntie Sadie, God rest 'er soul, once said the school kids hated 'im and the teachers 'ad no time for 'im. That's why he took that early retirement.'

Freda nodded in understanding, 'There'd not have been many at his funeral then, if they'd had it down there?'

'No, there'd have bin no one but Sadie and their family there. I remember her saying they had a memorial service for him at the school though.'

Cousin Freda gave a cynical smile, 'Well they had a captive audience for that didn't they?'

'We wouldn't 'ave gone all the way down there for

Don's funeral, would we Albert?' Auntie Agnes looked enquiringly across at her husband, who was examining a samosa with suspicion.

'No, nor this one, not wi' train fares the price they are.'

'Should be some baked 'am.' Uncle George was investigating the contents of the other offerings on the table. He pointed to a spring roll. 'What's that?'

'It's a spring roll, it has a vegetable filling, beansprouts, and all sorts of bits and pieces finely chopped.' James fancied himself a connoisseur of Chinese food. 'They're very tasty,' he added encouragingly.

'I'm not touchin' any o' them, they'll give me wind.' At last he spotted something familiar, 'Aye sausage rolls, that's more like it, pity they're such little uns.' He took three and retired to his armchair chuntering about "fancy tandadlings" as he eased himself into the seat.

'God give me strength!' muttered James as he and Marion sipped their coffee. 'How long will this go on for?'

'Until all the food's gone I should think. Despite the complaints they're like a flock of gannets.'

'Nobody's saying a word about your poor old mum; it's as if this isn't connected with her in any way,' James continued. Marion shrugged, 'As they say up here, "there's nowt so queer as folk."'

The conversations meandered on in a desultory fashion, with recollections about previous wakes, but little was mentioned about Sadie or her life. No one seemed to relate the event to the reason for it. Marion handed round the large plate of warm mince pies that had appeared on the table. When everybody had taken one she took the opportunity to talk to the childhood friends whom she'd heard her mother speak of but never met before.

'It was very good of you to come, especially on such a miserable day, and thank you for helping with the transport up here.'

'It were no trouble, and we had to pay our respects, didn't we Ivy?' Alice turned to her friend.

'Oh aye, we were all good pals when we were girls, before Sadie got married and went down south. Anyway, we never miss a funeral, do we Alice?'

Marion hid a smile and turned to back to the relative's camp, where Aunt Agnes confronted her, 'It seems your Sam couldn't make his Grandma's funeral then? Shame that.' Her face reflected her disapproval.

'No Auntie, he's at university in California on a year's exchange. We couldn't get him back here in time, and he had end of semester exams.'

'Hmm.' Agnes sniffed, 'semester indeed.' The feather on her hat wobbled as she shook her head.

'What else can I pass you Uncle George?' Marion turned to her uncle, anxious to avoid any more pointed remarks about her son's absence.

'I'll 'ave a few more of them there sausage rolls.' Marion obliged and filled the proffered plate with the last of the sausage rolls. 'What about a couple more salmon sandwiches and look, why not have another mince pie?' Anything to keep the old misery eating and stop the complaining. But Uncle George hadn't finished.

'We had sherry at our Bill's do,' he reminded everyone.

'Now, that's a good idea, why don't I get everyone

a sherry from the bar?' said James, swallowing his irritation at the family's lack of respect for his mother-in-law. There was a murmur of appreciative assent from the relatives.

'I'd rather have a pint of bitter,' said Uncle George.

'There's no pleasin' some folk.' This, sotto voce from Cousin Freda.

Marion wondered if alcohol would mellow the old grouches. The drinks were bought and handed round, and acid-drop faces sweetened a little.

'I think we need to raise a toast to Sadie,' proposed her husband.

'To Sadie,' they responded. 'To Mum,' said Marion, relieved things seemed to be taking a turn for the better.

'Aye that's a bit more like it,' said Uncle George, 'it's a pity there's no baked 'am nor fruit cake though. It's a poor do.'

'Just as well Sam couldn't get here,' muttered James to his wife, 'this lot would have driven him crazy.'

Eventually all that was left of the funeral baked meats were a few samosas and two spring rolls. Glasses were drained and the party was ready to be taken home. James and Marion ushered the relatives into the transport and returned them to their homes.

'Thank God that's over, it won't worry me if I never have to come up here again,' James sighed as they headed for the motorway.

'I'm not surprised Mum and Dad never came back after our grandparents died. With relatives like that, who needs enemies?' Marion tried to laugh but there was a catch in her voice. 'We were never particularly close, Mum and I, she was too buttoned up, never let her feelings show. I think I understand why now – it was that lot!'

'I still can't understand why your Auntie Agnes was so off-hand about her though, I mean, they were sisters for goodness sake.'

'Oh I think I know the reason for that,' Marion had regained her composure, 'Auntie Agnes fancied Dad herself once upon a time. I remember Mum once telling me that he had gone out with Agnes once before met her. I don't think she ever forgave Mum for being the sister he preferred.'

Orange

Di deWolfson

My hands' globe encloses yours,
receives your skin's pocked imprint
human, almost, as if through a microscope.

Warmth kindles your shy fragrance
holding back on bitterness, savouring
a long chain of associations,
jelly and ice treats and juice
only reluctantly, under pressure,
confessing to a hint of marmalade,
of cinnamon and Cointreau.

Oh the thrill of that first thumb-nail
exposing your creamy underskirt,
your fine pungent sneeze teasing
my nostrils' moist secrecy.
Patient, not peeling, I disrobe you
saliva all but dripping, teeth
like greedy children crowding
to the front.

Your flesh naked, my hunger lurches
into that first bite slavering sucking
your tissue ragged my cheeks flecked
stained my breath become orange.

This is your salvation
no slow burrowing decay
no rot nor wizening, this is
the ecstasy of death by desire.

Florence and Bill

An extract from a novel

Katrina Ritters

1917, Poplar, East London: Florence has just miscarried her baby. Her husband Frank is away fighting in the trenches.

Florence couldn't drag herself out of bed and lay there feeling a dreadful numbness, till way after her normal time. As she drifted in and out of sleep, the street sounds began to take on a different quality. Above the shrieks of the children and barking of dogs there had been a steady whine, followed by a thud. The sounds had stopped for a moment, then started up again, doubling in intensity. She could hear doors being slammed and people shouting to each other. When she went to the front door to look, there were people running down the street.

'Zeppelin raid, down at the school!' someone shouted out to her.

She dressed quickly, snatched up her gloves, carefully latched her front door behind her and stepped out into the road. Men and women were rushing past, shouting for others to join them, but she kept her own steady pace.

She saw the smoke first, as if from one of the factory chimneys of her northern childhood, dense and black over the tops of the terraced houses. There was a smell like fireworks after a display. The crowd grew thicker as she approached and now there were people heading away as well as towards the school on Upper

North Street. A couple walked towards her, their arms wrapped around each other, his hand pulling her head onto the rough shoulder of his jacket, his mouth set in a straight line, eyes blank and staring.

Then, before she was ready, the scene came into view. Fire engines, hoses spread across the pavement pouring water into a mass of smoke filled rubble. Dozens of people, mostly women, standing around. There was an eerie silence, apart from shouting – officials barking orders to stand back or get out of the way; desperate cries to fetch things or help carry away the wounded; sobbing, crying out in pain; a bell ringing in the distance.

She found herself pulled into the crowd, huddled against a makeshift barrier, kept back from the still-burning building. In a strange way she was able to take comfort from the grief and anxiety surrounding her, as if their grief could be for her loss too. A little way away she saw a face she recognised. One of the group of women who'd ignored her the other day was straining against the barrier, the lines on her face channelled even deeper by a furrowed brow and tight expression. A man came out of the building carrying a little girl, aged about eight, blood-stained and unable to walk. The woman let out a scream and moved forward to claim the child. The man, with big, calloused hands, hands that looked totally out of place on his thin body, probably a dockworker Florence thought, gently laid the girl on the ground and went back towards the smoking building.

'Wait' said Florence. 'Can I help? I can help.'

'You don't want to go in there. It's dangerous and we've more than enough casualties at the moment.'

But to Florence, physical injury, no matter how

bad, was a better option than the dull, unsettling grief that had nibbled away at her since the loss of her baby. Before anyone could protest she slipped under the rope designed to keep back the crowd and followed the dock-worker into the school.

Fortunately, the smoke and confusion were such that she was well inside the building before she was spotted. Once there, the sense of urgency and panic were such that no one was in a mood to turn away offers of help.

Inside what would have been the assembly hall there was a landslide of debris; pieces of brick, shards of glass, a painted blue coat hook, a piece of chalk, a buckled blackboard. Over it all hung a strange orange dust. Mingled with ash, this orange powder clouded Florence's hair, left a bitter taste on her lips. It frosted up-ended bricks in a kind of rosy light, hung like gold dust in the air. Above her, sparks flew into the sky as flames found a piece of wooden rafter. A fireman emerged from the debris, his oily face blackened with soot, and curious orange streaks where he had rubbed with his knuckles.

Underneath all this rubble, she knew, were the trapped forms of children. Some were dead already, others waited silently, waving a hand when they could summon the energy to appeal for help.

She moved closer to the man she'd seen earlier and saw him moving stones. She put on her gloves and, taking each piece he had removed, tossed it onto a pile of debris, to keep his working area clear. He was aware she was there but said nothing. After a while he said 'Give me a hand will you?' Together, they lifted a broken blackboard hiding a boy of about seven, grey school socks straining over what appeared to be a severed limb. Unconscious. Florence put her hand over her mouth to stifle her nausea.

The dock worker cradled the boy in his arms. With long, calloused fingers he gently picked away at the pieces of rubble on the boy's face, wiped away the dust from the boy's eyes with his handkerchief.

'Tell the ambulance-men where to come will you?' he said, without looking up.

But Florence was transfixed by the sight of his hands, stroking the boy's face. So gentle, but the hands were so rough, covered in nicks and scratches, callouses on the thumb. She stood and watched, seemingly unable to move, until the man said, still without looking up, 'Did you hear me? – we need to get this boy moved, but I can't do it on my own.'

So she pulled herself together and went to tell the ambulance-men where to come next. Outside a light drizzle was beginning to fall, orange sparks from those fires still burning standing out against the darkening sky. The crowd had dwindled now. Those parents that could, had claimed their children or followed them off to the hospital to see what could be done.

She was startled by the dock-worker and ambulance-man pushing past her, the young boy groaning on the stretcher. She stretched out her arm, wanting to hold the boy's hand, to give him some comfort, but they were hurrying now to get him into the ambulance. Now the pain of losing her own baby hit Florence once again. She thought of Margaret, having to endure the workhouse and the loss of her two children. How many children would die as a result of this bomb? And Frank – what would he be doing now?

Might he be trapped under rubble like these children? Might he be suffering and in pain? Might he be on his own or would there be someone there to comfort him?

She suppressed a shudder and then suddenly it became impossible to fight back tears. She slumped to the ground and held her head in her hands.

Before she knew it, the dock-worker was at her side, bending down and offering her a grubby handkerchief. The one he'd used to wipe the dust from the boy's eyes. Those hands again. She was fascinated by the number of cuts and scratches, the sheer size of the hands, compared to the long, thin body. She took the handkerchief dubiously, but after a while realised it was better than drying her tears on a sleeve.

'Thank you,' she said, blowing her nose.

'I told you not to come in, you should have stayed behind the barriers,' the man said. 'It's not surprising you're upset. You should go home.'

She opened her mouth as if to say 'it's not what you think' but closed it again. She couldn't face explaining, so she just nodded and turned to go.

'Wait a minute' he shouted after her 'I didn't catch your name'.

'Florence' she called over her shoulder. He came after her.

'Bill' he said, pointing at his chest.

13 Weston Road

Cashel Brook

It was the weekend and the weather was dry and unusually warm for early December as she took the M5 heading towards Bristol. This was not a planned trip that she had marked on some calendar or schedule, but it was an expected journey. Visiting her childhood home was something she had known she would have to do sooner or later, because in many ways it had been visiting her for a long time now. The three storey stone building would invade her mind in those quiet times of contemplation and its soft, ethereal footsteps had found a way to penetrate her dreams. Some of those dreams were pleasant but anxious, some of those dreams had been dark blankets of spiteful foreboding that wrapped her in the minutes, seconds and hours of a childhood that was mostly spent in trepidation and fear.

She wore sunglasses under her helmet to help her eyes against the low autumn sun. She cruised at an unhurried 60mph with her arms resting on the wheelbarrow handlebars and the steady vibration of the engine resonating through her body. She felt the uninterrupted cold of the motorway pierce her well prepared layers of clothing; much like the need for this trip had penetrated her pleasant and orderly life.

She swapped motorways from the M5 to the M4, preferring to enter Bristol by the more familiar route on the M32. She was taken aback by the rebuilding of the city centre and was forced to make a detour onto roads she had not planned on using. However she was still grateful that she recognised these roads and in finding more of Bristol was known than unknown. She rounded Cumberland Basin under the watchful presence of the Clifton Suspension Bridge and followed the dual carriageway to her exit.

As she entered the village of Long Ashton she started to feel that curious sensation that most adults feel when revisiting areas or homes that they associated with a time of distant childhood and adolescence. Everything seemed to be the wrong scale and too close together. Buildings and landmarks that had seemed bright and defined in memory now lay dull and ordinary in the light of an unremarkable autumn sun. But other memories, memories of times and experiences on these streets of this expansive village, those memories were bathed in the light of adventures, friendship and long sought after happiness. The memories of her childhood in this village could almost be defined by the time spent in her home and the time spent evading her home life, just as a growing flower might define its life between those hours spent in darkness and those in light.

The sound of her air cooled Honda's engine spoke and chattered in the narrow road that was boxed in on both sides with old stone walls. She enjoyed the throaty noise as if she was listening to the quiet chunterings of a giant that she knew on command could explode into roars and bellows of vigour and power. She had always loved the sound of her Honda CB650C and the bike was more a friend than a mere method of transport. It gave her a freedom and control in her life to go anywhere and the helmet and leathers gave her a comforting anonymity; on her bike she could be anyone heading to any destination.

She could feel her emotions begin to numb as she approached Weston Road, a gift she had resulting from her childhood at Number 13. She had the ability to suppress feelings of distress, anxiety, fear and similar emotions until they became just a small tight buzzing in her stomach. The vibrant sensation made her feel slightly nauseous and uneasy, but left her to think clearly and without much in the way of distraction from emotions that could otherwise overwhelm and confuse. The gift was as much a curse as it was a boon and she wondered, in a small disinterested way, if it was this gift that would always bring her back to this place in one way or another. She contemplated how the effects of a scar on flesh might restrict future movement or cause continuing discomfort and pain. More worryingly she deliberated if that same scar would always be a reminder of how it was acquired. She wondered if it was the same for mental scars and lesions and if, in time, they could be reduced to nothing more than a blemish. If indeed damage to the conscious or sub conscious could be reduced to something that was held by memory, but not regarded with significance or effect.

She stepped the bike down a gear and let it coast idly to a stop outside number 13 and ran through in her mind what she had planned to do. She had decided in a very orchestrated and contrived fashion to confront a part of her that she thought at one time, she could simply abandon and ignore. She had reasoned that she could simply rebuild her life and herself one step at a time and in the light of that rationale she had indeed stepped out of her past and into a brave new world. But it seemed that the uneasy foundations that she had built upon had begun to creak and groan under the weight of the many layers of belief, determination and attainment. The concrete thoughts that she had layered over the seeping mire of her childhood had begun to slip and shift, bringing doubt and cowed contemplation.

As she looked at the house she was amazed and yet haunted by how little it had changed. There had been changes to the windows with the addition of double glazing and a new front door. Someone had erected an ugly brick wall to block access to the driveway that led downwards to the basement and concreted area at the rear of the property. A similarly unattractive door led to the path that lay between the house and the driveway. But the house was eerily similar, too similar and she could easily see the child she had been coming towards her as she made her way back from school. The ghost of her childhood was dressed in plain black shoes and grey socks. Her grey skirt was knee length and her jumper was a faded navy blue. Her graffiti covered rucksack swung just above the ground, and she loosened her school tie as she went about her long practised post school ritual.

She would take the now gated path and trail her fingers along the cold, black handrail at the outside edge of the path. She watched in her mind's eye as the driveway dropped away as it sunk to the concrete courtyard behind the house. She passed through the metal gate at the end of the path and heard the familiar sound of friction passing through the metal hinges as it opened and then snicked closed again. She took the key from under a stone on the concrete ground floor balcony and let herself into the house. For a short time after each school day she was allowed the gift of being alone in the house and relished the uninterrupted quiet, feeling contentment in her isolation. She could almost feel the house in her memory stir from its slumber and reach through the years towards her.

She closed her eyes now and the child of her past walked past the door to the dining room on her right as she made her way from the back door and into the galley kitchen. Her finger tips investigated the cool, minutely dimpled surface of the breakfast bar that ran the kitchen's length as she paced its extent. The child paused before passing through the glass panelled door and into the hallway beyond. The three sections of panelled glass always gave her an uneasy feeling as its deeply patterned surface distorted the world beyond. She had always found that the distorted view that bent and twisted the world within its panes was the unsettling truth of the world and the view without its visual interference was the false reality. The door was pushed open and she allowed the curious feeling to pass as her mind lingered for a second on the cupboard under the stairs with its acutely angled door and faded white paint.

The front door was opposite her now with another door on her right leading to the living room and back to the dining room beyond. She walked to the front door and turned to face the stairs; she began to climb them. The carpet shimmered as her memory of its pattern changed and revised how she thought it should look. She found it surprising that she could not accurately recall its pattern after so many years of walking upon it. The first door, at the top of the stairs led into the chocolate brown bathroom and its bizarre and almost shameful colour made her smile. She recalled cold mornings and how she would fill the sink with hot water, before folding her arms and sinking them into the liquid heat that made goose bumps erupt across her body. She would stand there, the water rippling against her upper arms, caught in a strange sort of pleasure as she tried to push away the deep chill of the house and absorb as much of the restoring heat as she could.

The child left the bathroom and went next to her parent's room as it was the second door in sequence of four doors that led from the landing to the upstairs rooms. She could see the sunlight coming in from the rear facing window and the dust motes as they danced through the beams of illumination. The bed and a large wardrobe unit stood opposite each other in the centre of the room and an old treadle Singer sewing machine stood in the corner near the window. She let the child pass around the bed and approach the window. From this vantage she could see over houses and trees as the landscape fell away from the house and from here she could see all the way to the hill top village of Dundry in the far distance. She would often stand here and look into this expanse and let her mind drift in a simple unfocused way. As she steered the child to leave the room a chest of drawers appeared near the doorway. When she saw her mother's music box standing on its surface her memory continued to draw more of the past into the present.

The next door led to her brothers' room; they had shared a room that was separated by a kitchen unit. The bottom of the unit faced towards one bed and the top of the unit towards the other giving access to storage for each brother. A blue chest that had belonged to her grandfather lay at the bottom of one bed and shared drawers lay near another. Only one large window gave light to this room but the furniture arrangement effectively split the room in two, leaving one brother in light and the other in darkness. The young girl paused and she considered just how disturbingly prophetic that room's organisation had been. She stepped back onto the landing and took time to allow other details to emerge, such as the ceiling light and its flowery lampshade, the wood of the banister that separated the landing from the stairs and the strips of painted wood that made the loft hatch above her.

The child then at last came to her own bedroom and although the door was open she did not enter. The interior of this room was lost to a billowing and swirling darkness that seemed to have an acrid sentience. For the first time she became aware that the child could smell her surroundings and the scent that she had detected could only be described as despair. Even the smell of that room gave rise to feelings and memories that she was not yet prepared to explore or even acknowledge. She kept the room and all that it meant or could ever mean, locked away, even from herself. She had consigned that room and all of its memories to a void in her mind where restless images warped and twisted as they tried to make themselves real and meaningful once more. The girl of her memory may not have been strong enough to do this, but the adult mind that resided behind the child's eyes was practiced, deliberate and sure. The woman simply turned away and walked back down the stairs.

She walked through the lounge and dining room and she took her time to remember them as they had once been at one time or another. The woman left by the back door, turned the key in the lock and placed it back under the stone, effectively sealing away the main part of the house before she turned and made her way over to the steps. She stood atop the concrete steps that led from the ground floor balcony to the garden level and basement below. She felt the nausea and the vibrations in her stomach increase as she both wanted to descend the stairs and run from them at the same time. She could almost see the shadows that would be waiting for her down there as they competed for her fear and regret. She held the rail that bordered the pathway, balcony and these steps and felt the familiar coolness of the black painted metal.

As she started to descend the steps, carefully, one step at a time as if approaching a dreaded and resented enemy, a different kind of coolness passed through her. It was if her foe was some matted, ravaged animal that lay sleeping and all but the most considered of approaches would lead to its waking. The girl appraised the thirteenth step; its uneven surface had been responsible for both sudden descents and failed ascents. As she reached the thirteenth step at the rear of number 13 Weston Road she stopped and tightened her grip on the rail. Her eyes carefully and gradually slid to the black double doors of the basement level. The paint was peeling in places and one door had an arc missing at the bottom of its opening edge where her brother's long deceased rabbit had gnawed its way through. Soft light crept inwards to all the things that lay beyond in her most hated and feared of places in this house. Without thought, without consciously allowing it, she saw a foot pass by the interior of the breach. Something had crept into the carefully planned visitation of her former home and the girl haunting the steps stiffened. There came a shout, as loud and angry as it was insensible. It came from behind the basement doors and this was followed by the unmistakable sound of flesh connecting hard with flesh. As her heart began to descend further than any steps could take her, she heard first the yelp and then the scream of a dog.

The woman should have reacted as the hidden truths of her past tried to force their way out of that detestable place to overwhelm her. Instead an iron will slammed into the basement and all of its contents were turned black as it was enveloped by a deep, swirling smoke. She placed the basement and all it contained back into the void from which it was trying to escape. The woman held her chin up high, regarding the basement doors with an appraising look, but not a fearful one. The girl she had been had yet to come to terms with what was happening in this house, but the woman had both accepted her past and overcome it. But she still knew that, one step at a time, she would also have to face her past, or a part of her would forever remain the girl perching on the thirteenth step too scared to go forwards and too regretful to go back. She turned and ascended the stairs.

As she walked back along the path at the side of the house she began to grow and mature. By the time she reached the end of the path she was a woman once more. Her school jumper and skirt had been replaced with a thick brown leather jacket and protective padded motorcycle jeans. The unsure, nervous features of the perpetually fearful girl had become the steady gaze of an expressive woman that possessed confidence and courage.

She opened her eyes and looked out from behind her sunglasses, she felt the steady reassuring rhythm of the 4 cylinder engine as it idled. She selected a gear and then checked over her shoulder before pulling away. She might visit this place again from time to time, but she felt that its hold on her would lessen in the coming years. She would face everything that the house held for her, she would face it one memory at a time until everything was placed and no shadows remained. It would then fade into the mists of memory and time, just like the pattern of the carpet she could not quite remember.

The December air chilled her face as she found the bypass and felt the thrill as she opened the throttle. The world began to blur with the speed of her passing and a feeling of freedom filled her being. In return it pushed away the emotions of her formative years as they were consigned once again to her own inner basement. The future rushed towards her.

See No Evil

Mark Bradbury

'Are you sure you'll be alright Dad?'
'Yes, don't worry about me love, I'll wait here for you to come back after you've been over the road.'

Bob Davies made the trip to the bank every Friday morning to pay a few bills and take a bit of cash out to see him through until the following week. It was a bit of a routine but it worked well for him and he'd done it for several years.

'I'll see you to the end of the queue and I promise I won't be longer than fifteen minutes. Don't start walking home on your own but wait for me, ok? There's a chair just inside the door, I'll meet you there.'

'Yes, now you go off, don't worry about me Susan love, I'll be fine, I come here every week; I know it like the back of my hand.'

Susan Chambers nevertheless *did* worry about her Dad. He wasn't in the best of health but since he'd lost his wife he was determined to carry on regardless and Susan was very proud of him. Bob usually managed to walk the quarter of a mile or so to the village by himself and he knew his way around very well. Today, Susan had taken the day off work and wanted to spend some time with her father, but she had to get a prescription from the Chemist before they closed for lunch.

Bob was ex-army and had worked in the bomb squad for nearly fifteen years until an accident led to his retirement and a much less physically active job for the remaining twenty years of his working life. Bob had also been a part-time PT instructor and had boxed for his regiment, winning several belts along the way.

He waited patiently in the queue just as he did every week, slowly shuffling forward as each person was served. Eventually his turn came at the counter.

'Hello Mr Davies, how are you this morning?' the young woman behind the counter asked.

'Not too bad thank you, the weather certainly feels nice and warm today.'

'I know, it looks lovely out there too; I just hope it lasts, I'm hoping to have a barbecue with a few friends this evening. Anyway, what can I do for you today?'

'Well, there's a gas bill to pay and I'd like my usual seventy pounds in tens please,' Bob said as he passed the gas bill and cheque under the glass partition.

'No problem Mr Davies.' The bank clerk took the gas bill and cheque and processed it, completing the transaction by counting out seven ten pound notes. 'Your bill's paid and there's your money; is there anything else I can help you with today?'

'No that's fine, thank you my dear,' Bob said, picking up the money and putting it in his wallet. 'Good morning.'

'Good bye, see you next week Mr Davies.'

Bob started to make his way towards the door only to be pushed roughly aside by a group of balaclava-clad men bursting through the door of the bank.

'Stay still, shut up and no-one will get hurt!' one of the men shouted, waving a sawn off shot gun around. 'You! Behind the counter, put as much cash as you have from your desks and the safe in these bags!' The man shoved a couple of large cloth bags over the counter to one of the clerks. 'And don't even think about raising the alarm!'

The other men milled around menacingly, one waving a length of metal pipe and the other a baseball bat whilst the bank clerk busily stuffed packets of notes into the bags and kept looking nervously at the man doing all the talking and brandishing the gun.

'Stop wasting time and get on with it, I'll use this thing if I have to, I really will.' He was scanning the now very frightened customers in the bank with the gun whilst his two colleagues strode around watching, waiting and threatening.

Bob was still close to the entrance door where he had been pushed aside and was wondering what to do; his mind flashed back to his younger days and he remembered how he wouldn't have thought twice about taking matters into his own hands but he knew now that his health was against him.

Within a minute or two the bags were stuffed full of cash but the clerk seemed unsure what to do next and looked very frightened.

'Throw them over the top – hurry up!' The girl threw the bags over the glass partition and Baseball Bat grabbed them.

The men made one last sweep of the staff and customers as if to warn them not to move and then they began to make their escape through the door.

Bob had made his mind up and it was now or never; he was back in the army and his training kicked in.

As the last man pushed his way past Bob through the door, he grabbed the man's jacket and pulled him back into the bank. Using all the strength he had, he tried to over-balance him and push him to the floor. Bob succeeded in pulling the balaclava off, but couldn't get the man off his feet. He felt a heavy blow to the back of the head and nothing else.

***

'Mrs Chambers is here, Sarg, to identify her father,' the Police Constable said, popping his head into the office behind the reception counter of Basingstoke Mortuary. On that fateful day Susan had returned to collect her father from the bank, only to be met by much commotion, police and ambulance men milling around with Bob lying in the bank in a pool of blood.

'Hello Mrs Chambers, my name's Sergeant Blewitt and I'm the Family Liaison Officer for Basingstoke Police. If you're ready, please follow me.' The Sergeant took Susan through to one of the back rooms where a body lay covered with a sheet.

Sergeant Blewitt nodded to the mortuary technician who very carefully pulled the sheet from the body. He asked, 'Mrs Chambers, is this your father Robert Davies?'

'Yes,' she said quietly, unable to hold back her tears as she turned away and buried her face in her hanky. It hadn't been long since she had found her mother on the kitchen floor after suffering a major stroke and now this. It was just too much to bear.

'Please accept my sincere condolences, Mrs Chambers,' Sergeant Blewitt added and gestured to the technician to replace the cover over Bob Davies.

Susan was now a little more composed. 'What happened? He was a harmless, elderly widower who wouldn't hurt a fly.'

'From witness statements from customers and staff in the bank and the CCTV, it looks like your father tried to intervene as one of the gang members left the premises. He managed to pull the balaclava off him and one of the others used his weapon on your father.'

'But why did they have to kill him? They could have just pushed him to floor; knowing Dad, he might have had a go at them but surely they could see he was no *real* threat to them.'

'Well, a couple of witnesses say the gang member who lost his balaclava turned around and your father looked directly at him. We think the other man was worried your father could identify him and decided to stop him in the only way he knew. It was all a bit pointless really because they must have known about the entrance CCTV; we have a nice clear shot and we've been able to identify him.'

'I'll say it was pointless, he…..' At which point Susan started sobbing again and the rest of the sentence faded away.

'I'm sure we'll have them apprehended soon, Mrs Chambers; armed robbery is bad enough but added to that, cold blooded murder of a defenceless old man and they'll throw away the key.'

'You don't get it, do you?' shouted Susan; her sobbing had subsided and she was angry now and shaking uncontrollably.

'Can I get you a nice cup of tea, Mrs Chambers?'

The sergeant tried to smile but was beginning to look a little confused.

'He wouldn't have recognised his own family a few inches in front of his nose. After a faulty hand grenade blew up in his face when he was in the army, he was virtually blind. He didn't have his white stick with him because *I* was there that day and he didn't need it.'

Susan was shouting and deeply upset now. 'Don't you see? They didn't *need* to kill him and if I hadn't taken the day off, they might have realised and he'd still be alive.'

Sandra. RIP

Kay Howles

When I woke up, I knew it was the thirteenth of August and I knew it was a Friday. However, that wasn't what actually struck me about the day. What struck me was that I knew I was dead. Not at that moment because at that moment I was still alive and I was thinking what I was thinking. But I knew it was the end of my life, or at least the beginning of the end, because I am not a stupid woman, whatever some might think.

I am a private woman who would rather think than speak and I knew I could never speak about this. Something was wrong, very wrong. Something was broken and could not be fixed. I didn't need any doctor or Wikipedia article to give me this news. I just knew that part of me had stopped working. It wasn't my heart which some say can be broken in two. It wasn't my brain which sometimes fails you when you need it most. It was an organ, a corporeal organ that my body could not survive without. Most would probably wonder what this organ was and more importantly what it did to ensure that life went on. I knew these things because, as I said, I am not a stupid woman. I knew very well that I would not see another thirteenth of August. I knew I would not see another Friday the thirteenth because, being a superstitious person, I knew that this was my Friday the thirteenth.

I am not the first person that this has happened to.

I know that I will ultimately become a statistic and I don't really fancy that. I would rather die in complete anonymity because, as I've already told you, I am a private person. I was happy with being that in life and will be happy with it in death. There are those that I love and will leave behind. They will be bereft but that cannot concern me now because I did not choose this, it chose me. So I lie hear listening to the rain as it taps incessantly on the roof of the caravan and I think about choice. A choice that is mine and mine alone. I can decide to make today the day I go to my creator or I can wait and let the drugs and experts decide which day it will be. What shall I do?

'So where are we going?'
    'I told them at your office.'
    'Oh right, I will just check then.'

'Are you sure that's where you want to go?'
    'Not really, but I have to.'
    'You are very brave.'
    'How so?'
    'Well, people don't usually go if they have a choice.'
    'Ergo, I don't have a choice.'
    'Well, I have taken people who had a choice there before.'
    'Did any of them come back?'
    'Some of them.'
    'Did you bring them?'
    'Yes, it would always be me; I am the only one who does this run.'

'Why are we stopping?'
'Engine trouble, I'll just take a look, shouldn't take long.'

'Is everything okay?'
'Yes, it's fine. Do you want to keep going or shall we go back?'
'There is nowhere to go back to.'
'You know that isn't true.'
'If I don't go now I will have to go on another day.'
'So what's wrong with going then, what's your hurry?'
'I want to choose when I go, I don't want someone else to decide.'
'I have to remind you that you haven't been invited.'
'I didn't think I had to be, I thought I could go any time.'
'Unexpected arrivals are never welcome.'
'How do you know that?'
'I told you that I have taken some of them back.'
'Did they ask you to take them again?'
'Some did.'

'I'll just pull over here for a minute.'
'Why, engine trouble again?'
'No I always get to where I'm told to go eventually.'

'How much longer are we going to stay here?'

'Until you tell me to carry on.'

'I think I'll go back.'
   'Good idea.'

'I'll phone you when I need you then.'
   'I'll come and take you as soon as you're invited.'

So that was my choice. I let them try to fix me even though I knew it was just a small sticking plaster on a gaping wound that needed innumerable stitches. I knew that all there was, was time, mostly spent in pain, time that would not be measured by me and time with every second spent in fear. What difference did that extra time make to me and others? Time spent alone in my own waiting room, clutching a one-way ticket that had no date on it. A ticket I wanted to tear into a thousand pieces and scatter on the ground. A ticket that was there every time I opened my purse. A ticket that I hadn't bought. I waited for him to come back for me, not knowing when that would be and hoping it would be on a better day, albeit such days were few. I waited for my invitation to arrive, often wondering if it had been lost somewhere because I knew it had been posted on Friday the thirteenth of August.

'I wasn't expecting you today.'
   'Oh I think you were.'
   'How did you know to come?'
   'The office told me.'
   'What if I don't want to go now?'
   'You've been invited; it would be rude not to turn

up.'

'How long will it take?'
'We are already there.'

'So this is it then?'

'Yes. Those who left before are there to welcome you; you will have a wonderful time.'

'What if I don't want to see everyone?'

'Then they won't be there. The choice is yours. It will always be yours now.'

The Sergeant's Speech

Derek Miller

At this passing out parade
with lots of gleaming braid
I know you will have prayed
to check you made the grade.
You have already been assessed
We are looking for the best.
The critical final test
to see if you're well-dressed.

Don't worry about the fight,
you must look good in any light
In trouble, just use your phones
when dealing with unknowns
if necessary we'll send drones
no use risking your bones.
Civilians die in any war
soldiers aren't killed any more.
But you need to wear Dior
and be future DNA store.

After conflict we need
people to breed
how to succeed
and then to lead.
The questions are on style

a difficult trial
see how you beguile
with a smile.

Now I need you to walk
proud like a peacock
tread carefully round the block
with looks that would knock
out any pretender
you have to be slender
and be a contender
so people will surrender.

So let's start the boogie
no need to be heavy duty
it's your duty
to show off booty.
For those that don't pass
just by looking crass
you're out on your ass
treated like outcast,
or worse as a civilian
chance one in a million.

Note: Patterns in conflict: from UNICEF. Civilians are now the target. Civilian fatalities in wartime have climbed from 5 per cent at the turn of the century - to more than 90 per cent in the wars of the 1990s.

A Special Visit

Dave Griffiths

On the dark oak table, polished through the ages by countless hands, lay the Book opened at the page Jeremiah had been seeking. It was the Good Book, in such families the only book in the house. The King James Bible had been the property of his dear wife's family for the last three hundred years, and just lately, he had often sought comfort and explanation from it.

"The Heavens declare the glory of God and the firmament sheweth his handy worke." It didn't say enough to satisfy him.

It had been over a month since anyone had seen Jacqueline Mountenay in the little town, about the same time that Jeremiah had not got drunk in his favourite bar. He was hard to miss when he came into town; he was lacking somewhat in the social niceties of behaviour, but some people prey on simple folks' weaknesses. Now you could see Jeremiah every day and night from the roadside on his porch sitting in his rocking chair, with his shotgun on his lap. No one waved: he would have only looked past them anyway.

The first time Sheriff Dean came round to ask about her he wasn't satisfied. Jeremiah was well known. 'People be'n talking, Jeremiah,' said the Sheriff.

'Someone be'n talking.' Some neighbour I have! Me? A wife-beater? If he ever says that again I'll kill him an' I mean it!' Said a purposeful Jeremiah in his slow and lazy Louisiana drawl.

But tongues will always find exercise for, after all, Jeremiah was fifty four, and his pretty little wife was only thirty five. There were always problems of a sexual nature when a man showed more interest in the bottle than the flesh, and he never did say where she was. And then the Sheriff's wife said she had this dream and it was "kinda spooky" but she was often right, for then still more people asked after little Jacky.

No local sheriff's office could handle it and so finally, they sent down a police Lieutenant and a team from Baton Rouge some fifty miles upstate to sort things out on a special visit. Jeremiah was calm. They exchanged 'Howdies'.

'We come to search the place Jeremiah. We have a warrant from the D.A.' said Sheriff Dean. Jeremiah did not seem moved.

'We'd appreciate it if you'd cooperate, Mister Mountenay. Ain't no need to get upset about things,' said Lieutenant Dominart, usually an impressive man to simple country folk.

'Ya'll only find one missin' nightgown an' one missin' pair of shoes. Ya'll find she packed no bags. She just gone. I'm a pretty smooth investigator myself,' drawled Jeremiah. 'Well, I ain't just got no story sayin' she'd left to see her sister. I be'n over the facts myself time and time again, but I have no answers. She just gone one night an' I ain't seen her since.' Both the Sheriff and the Lieutenant went inside along with the three men from Forensics. 'Ya'll find I'm a simple soul an' I have nothin' to hide.' He closed the opened Bible. 'This Bible is English. My wife's kinfolk came a long time ago from

England. But it's a miserable comfort at times like this.' The whole place was ramshackle and he seemed embarrassed by that fact. 'My daddy had a thousand acres. It's all sold off now 'cept for three fields and this farmhouse. As ya know it's my neighbour who owns everythin' round here. Now he wants this too.' Jeremiah sighed. 'My kinfolk were French Huguenots; my great, great, great, great granddaddy came here to escape persecution well over two hundred years ago. Seems that'll never stop.'

Lieutenant Dominart gave instructions to his team and left them to it. Although the place was dirty, the furniture was impressive and Dominart was a man of taste and sophistication, especially in the way a man can look if he can pay for it. He was of French extraction himself after all, and to the women he looked real cute with his little moustache and cultivated manners. For him it was always a pleasure to be able to recognise quality. He was the sort of man Jacky Mountenay would have found attractive. He smoothed his hand over the table.

'My great, great granddaddy bought that table and chairs from France. Had 'em shipped across. He forgave too easily. He loved everythin' from France,' said Jeremiah.

'C'est seulement les Francais qui savent bon gout,' prompted Dominart.

Jeremiah did not understand and could not respond of course except with an excuse. 'Times are hard. I ain't got nothin' left. But maybe I don't need nothing.' Dominart picked up a photo of the missing wife with Mountenay but made no comment. 'The Good Lord never blessed us with children. I never ever said His name for years, but I'm a reformed man now,' said a thoughtful Jeremiah.

'Just here to do my work Mr Mountenay,' said Dominart. He saw that she did look pretty, a real showdog like the Sheriff had told him.

'Yar men look real busy over there. They won't find a darn thing,' said a smiling Jeremiah. 'See them Sheriff, real slow an' careful they are, but there ain't nothin' to find.'

The Forensics team systematically searched each room, their shoes and hands covered in plastic mitts. Dominart spoke to each of them in turn. Every room had its own history, and every crime scene told its own story. They would find everything they needed, but they had to be careful about what was admissible as evidence. They were there to reconstruct crime scenes and identify the person or persons responsible for criminal acts, and Dominart was sure a crime had been committed. The team made a hundred sketches and plans, took a hundred different samples from each room in the house and took what seemed like a thousand different camera shots from every angle of every room to extract a thousand different clues. They would recognize the scene and document the scene looking for blood to date and type. Everything was tagged, logged and then packaged up. It was logic and applied science, but there seemed to be no traces of blood, and there had been no disinfectant used in that household in years to mask the smell of death. There was nothing obvious, but hard work was the key and so they went out to the front of the house, and then to the barn and then the fields and started the process over again and again.

'It's real important Sheriff,' said Dominart out of earshot of Jeremiah, 'to be thorough. I'll tell the team this ain't no time to commune with nature. I believe this man was capable of chopping his wife into little pieces. We'll find out. It's the twenty first century and we'll find out. I've had fifteen years of experience in these matters. We'll have something when it's analysed. I know I'm right. I study body language. I am almost an expert in non-verbal communication. He don't fool me!'

The Sheriff took a walk down to the shallow creek. There was no noise and there were no birds. There was the smell of drought and the smell of singed earth. It was summer, but there seemed to be no insects. All he found was a large, perfectly circular area of scorched earth. He brought over the Lieutenant.

'Some kind of funeral pyre?' posited Dominart. 'Jeremiah scraped away the ashes?'

'Another of yar theories?' asked the by now unimpressed Sheriff Dean. 'Why not just put her in the incinerator in the barn Lieutenant?'

'I've been speakin' to him. Quotes the Bible too often to act rational,' said Dominart. He did not want to give offence so he did not ask if there was much of a history of inbreeding round those parts.

They searched the three fields for the signs of freshly disturbed earth and soon they would have to do the same for the creek, but that was shallow, and Mountenay had no boat and anyway she'd be too easy to find in that water. But time was the key to a confession and so he decided he'd go back to the little town and let Jeremiah chew on things overnight. He called the suspect over.

'Mr Mountenay, you were a jealous man!' said the Lieutenant.

'Ya're real serious aren't ya?' responded Jeremiah. 'I know what ya thinkin', but we had nigh on twenty years together an' I wanted more. If we had problems, we sorted them out ourselves in our own time,'

'I do not have the patience of a saint, Jeremiah,' said Sheriff Dean. 'Ya have a temper on ya as I know well.'

'That was before. This gen'leman now before ya does not lower himself to fist fightin,' said Jeremiah.

'Jeremiah, I'm looking at ya straight in the eye. Stop joshin' now, ya have a criminal conviction for aggravated assault,' replied the Sheriff.

'Your wife was very pretty Mr Mountenay,' said the Lieutenant.

'My wife was a real lady who I treated with respect. It's people like yah who show the same old human weaknesses. Yar thoughts only tell me ya indulge in experiences which do not separate man from the beasts,' retorted Jeremiah.

'Jeremiah,' said Sheriff Dean, 'ya are doin' yaself no good in what ya're sayin'.'

'Ask me real nice, sheriff, and I still can't tell ya any different. I try to greet each day with a smile and the Lord's Prayer. If I done what ya thinkin', I'd be afraid to close my eyes at night. She just gone an' I'm entitled to hope for a new start.' He looked right at Dominart. 'Do ya ever wish ya had another life, mister detective? I sure do. Old age can be worse than death, Lieutenant Dominart.'

Dominart was unmoved.

'Just one more question Mr Mountenay. You only got the pickup truck?' asked Dominart. Mountenay nodded. Dominart had already disabled the starter motor; Mountenay was going nowhere after they'd left him. Then he thought of the photos of him and his little wife; she seemed in those to have had no fun at all with this man. The motive was still obvious to him. 'Your wife was an attractive woman,' he repeated.

'She was, I know. She sometimes used to wear perfume and powder. It was against God's law, but then I saw no harm in it,' said Mountenay. 'It ain't no big secret. But ya know it was my wife who had the strongest faith.'

It was nearly nine in the evening when the lawmen drove the ten miles back to town.

'Our Jeremiah is not as dumb as he looks. If he was wearin' a sad face when he told me that story, then maybe I'd 'a believed him,' said a depressed Lieutenant Dominart. 'Plausible and cunning he is not. I don't suffer fools or drunks gladly. If I had my way, at least he'll do life for doing this. Should go to the chair really. Madness....age no defence in my opinion.'

This all seemed to be turning into a massive embarrassment all round. Dominart in truth believed they had nothing. With no eye witnesses, they couldn't say too much about things they may have believed but couldn't prove. The truth may never come out.

'He's as crazy as a loon. Be'n crazy for years,' said a despondent Sheriff Dean. 'Twenty years of marriage was the miracle. Same with me I suppose. Wife of mine gets an idea into her head an' my imagination runs away with me. I'm tired. Just need to hit the hay.'

Dominart lay back and looked up through the windscreen to the sky. The skies they got round there were incredibly beautiful. There was no light pollution. Every so often a minute meteor would streak across it. It was the time of the Perseids, and the Lieutenant smugly told himself that he would be the only man in that whole county who would be aware of that fact, and that amongst these people those streaks in the skies would be the stuff of yet another unexplained mystery, local legend or piece of folklore to explain a simple example of celestial magic. In the morning they would pull Mountenay in, fruitlessly question him, then release him without charge. He'd then go back to civilization in Baton Rouge.

Now Jeremiah opens the Bible, and reads it in the light of one forty-watt bulb on the porch. What he wants is not there in the Book.

Hebrews 13:4. *"Marriage is honorable in all, and the bed undefiled: but whoremongers, and adulterers God will judge."*

He feels that's not enough to stop real hard questions about any true believer's faith. There has not been a single day he hasn't thought about her. He hasn't gone into the bedroom for three weeks. He don't want no bad dreams no more. In his heart he's still married to her, but it's not a true heart that he has. He is not looking at atonement.

Explaining that he had not killed his wife to any police officer had been impossible. Where there's no sense to any of it there can be no understanding. He thinks that maybe God has a plan for our salvation? Maybe it is in the nature of man to dream of the impossible? He's maintained an around the clock watch on the very spot that he last saw her. They might return tonight.

Weeks ago, on 21st June, something had happened. The Government knows all about it. Jeremiah knows it's all on record. It was like nothing he'd ever seen before. Surely there were loads of calls; someone must have seen it too. There must have been hundreds of reports of strange lights across the County.

An apparition? An illuminated shape suspended in the sky? There was so much heat and so much light. There was no sound. It come over the house, across the barn to the creek; a sort of sphere ten feet over the creek. It stopped; it hovered over the water. Jacky was in a sort of trance when it landed in the back field. There were no screams from her. She was calm when she went with them. She had no fear but he was too frightened. Did he cry? No! But he sure didn't want to die!

Then it rose in a circle of intense white light. When it took off it left no vapour trail but the heat killed all life there on the ground and it has not come back. The birds and insects know something we don't. Then the spaceship disappeared. It was gone in a few seconds. The speed was incredible. How could he tell them that aliens had landed in a spaceship and then gone away with his wife? He'd never reported her missing. He was sorry now he hadn't gone with her, but there have been a few signs already that they might return tonight.

Now it's not right for a man of simple faith like him to question anything in the Book. Is this all because she had decided to sell her soul to the devil? He often thinks how precious life is but right now he feels he wants to never have to live another day in his wicked world. It's not been a good life while it's lasted. He wants to shut his eyes and burst into flames for there is no goodness in this world.

He reloads the shotgun once more. He can't use it on them and maybe he knows he can't ask for her back. But he knows he'll have to decide on everything by himself before the morning comes and Lieutenant Dominart returns.

The Big Issue

Paul Chiswick

The alarm clock's shrill ringing carves Aija's sleep. Half-awake, she throws off the thin blankets, swings her aching legs over the metal bed rail and flicks on the single, naked bulb hanging from the centre of the nicotine-stained ceiling. The windowless room smells of perfume and damp.

Her home spans but two single beds and a dilapidated chest of drawers crushed between them. Inside the top drawer, neatly folded, lie the clothes she wears to sell *The Big Issue*; black headscarf, crocheted cap, voluminous gypsy skirt that hangs to mid-calf, white cotton shirt, and thick red socks.

She has come to hate every single item.

'Wear your traditional costume, Aija,' they said. 'People here find that very appealing.'

She objected, arguing she only wore such clothes on rare occasions.

'Take it from us, you need to stand out. You won't sell any magazines if you don't.'

She reaches under the bed and pulls out a well-worn knapsack. At the bottom lies a battered tin. She takes it out, prises off the lid and spreads crumpled banknotes and a single photograph on the bed. The photograph is of her husband before his accident at the factory left him in a wheelchair. She counts the notes and shakes her head, wondering if it was a mistake to leave her homeland. At this rate, it will be many years before Georgs and she make love again and little Mikelis hugs his absent mother. By that time her son will have changed so much he probably won't know who she is.

The bed opposite has a pair of silk stockings draped over its foot and she feels a burning need to touch them. She slides her feet into her slippers, crosses the narrow space and takes a stocking in her hand: smooth, sensuous, Velna's. They arrived in Birmingham on the same day, discovered they were both from Riga, and decided to share a place. The girl isn't beautiful, not by a long way. But it isn't her face men want and Aija imagines she learned long ago how to make full use of what God gave her. No way would Velna be seen holding a magazine in her hand, passers-by looking down the length of their noses at her, narrowed eyes telegraphing their disdain.

'I will be in this country two years, no more, Aija. Then I will go back and buy a place in Riga.'

'But how Velna? How will you do this?'

A man called Stanislaw began to call for Velna. Polish, tall, smartly dressed. Polite, friendly.

'Who is Stanislaw, Velna?'

'My....employer.'

'You never said you have work.'

'I must have forgotten.'

'What kind of work?'

'Work that pays well, Aija. You should try it.'

She glances at her watch. In half an hour Stanislaw will arrive to drop off Velna and collect her.

She sighs, begins to roll the stocking up her leg.

It is time to go to her new job.

The Reunion

Anne Santos

Oh God! I thought, what had possessed me to suggest a reunion. I sighed as I parked the car in the car park and walked slowly round to the front entrance of the wine bar. How simple it had all sounded ten years ago as the four of us sat at the corner table of the small wine bar laughing and giggling. We'd drunk a bottle or three of wine and then raised our glasses and wished each other well – 'Keep in touch' – 'Oh yes, we must keep in touch!' And then probably due to the wine and the false bonhomie atmosphere I'd said, 'Oh we really should keep in touch, why don't we all meet here in ten years time! Same time, same date...'

Of course they had all agreed 'What a super idea.' I'd smiled round the group. Beth at twenty-four was the youngest and thought she was definitely going places. We all envied her, she was so pretty with fair-hair and baby-doll blue eyes. She was nice but not too smart or intelligent, but she got the men with her baby-doll appeal...oh yes, Beth was going places.

Gina, who was really Jean, but who had decided Gina sounded more glamorous and fitted her image, although no one quite knew what image she wished to portray, was two years older than Beth. She was of mixed-race, attractive in a positive way, tall and amusing with a chip on her shoulder that caused her to give snide remarks if she felt she was being threatened. Then Melanie – the oldest at twenty-nine, was determined to find that man who could give her the luxuries of life. She put herself about, a boob-job – facials, short skirts, the lot. We all envied her the courage to go under the knife for vanity.

Now, come to think of it, I didn't have much in common with any of them. Well, we didn't have much in common with each other, we weren't friends. Okay, we'd worked in the same office, laughed and joked, the usual – semi camaraderie stuff, but it was surface, no depth – they didn't know me, anymore than I knew them.

We'd always had an end of week Friday evening drink. Lots of ribald humour, and the usual office gossip. Who'd been in the stationery cupboard with "handy-hands Harry". He liked to think of himself as a real lothario whereas he was just a "masher". Jeremy with his fantasy stories and floppy hair, all talk, no action as I found out. Then Bill the bore who had hollow legs when it came to beer drinking. Wee Jamie…he's gay, you know? Is he? And then there was Edward who we all thought of as a dork. We'd all teased Edward – no matter how he tried, and try he did, he could not fit in. He was always on the outside of the groups, the outside when we had the occasional night out at the pub. He'd tag along, pay for drinks, laugh too loudly at jokes he didn't find amusing, 'Poor Eddy' we'd all say, because try as he would, and try he did, he was in the end the man who could not fit in. We'd all agreed then he wasn't bad looking, dressed well and he was clever…just an unsociable bore.

So ten years ago, we'd all worked together and then suddenly it had fragmented – the company – bought over, redundancies, voluntary and otherwise. We'd all decided it was time to move on.

I was off to London; at twenty-four it was time I moved on. No reason, only someone I knew had a flat and well, it made sense to me at the time not to hang around. I was ambitious, no brain box but street-wise, no beauty but a sense of humour and purpose which carried me through so you could ignore my plainness. So, the pact was, we wouldn't email or make any contact, we'd just meet up here ten years on.

Of course, I was the first to arrive, I looked round at the now garish wine bar, ten years on it had changed, but I guess so had we. I sat down at the corner table and ordered a coffee, went to light a cigarette and remembered the law told me I couldn't smoke now over a drink! I crossed a jeaned leg over the other; perhaps I should have dressed a little less casual – trainers, jeans and a sweat shirt…ah well!

We'd nothing in common ten years ago, what the hell would we have now – I wished I hadn't come, I could have put my time to better use. So here I was sitting at the corner table – glass and glitter music by an unknown group blaring away, drinking coffee. I saw the taxi pull up outside and blinked at the woman who now staggered in.

'Lynn.'

I heard the voice and stood up to be squashed in the folds of flesh and ample bosom. Bleary eyes beneath layers of eye-shadow and thinly plucked eyebrows and a mop of glitzy yellow hair. 'My God, you've not changed,' watery eyes scanned me with resentment.

'Beth!' I wished I could say the same but I was shocked by her appearance. She sat down and immediately ordered a large glass of house-red and peered at me and proceeded to talk non-stop in a nervous chatter.

'So you came?' I glanced up hearing the drawl and saw a slim elegant woman in a mask-like face. 'Gina.' We hugged and my nostrils took in the aroma of Opium. As we sat down, she looked me up and down. 'You could have dressed a little more elegantly,' she still had a brittle tongue. 'But you always did manage to look...' she hesitated and Beth cut in

'Casual!'

Melanie arrived late; she looked tired and pregnant. She refused wine or coffee and asked for bottled water. We heard she had four children, oh yes she was married, that was her life. 'For God's sake,' Gina snapped, 'keep your legs shut...'

We settled down into dilatory conversation. Beth consumed glass after glass of red wine, she was unhappy, her life a mess, divorced twice, she was on the road to alcoholism. Gina was pure professional something or other, cool and resentful, her skin so stretched she could barely smile whilst one eye seemed to point north and the other south. Melanie was just drowning in kids but happy.

We then started the *whatever happened to?* Bill, they had heard he'd married and stopped drinking, Harry, he had a wife and girl-friend, James had come out. Oh, and that dork – Edward?' Melanie said, 'Can you believe it, he's tipped for a knighthood, good work and all that. He's made an absolute fortune in property!'

As we tried to go back ten years and find some common ground, a waiter, I use the term lightly, came across to the table. 'Anyone own a red Porsche?'

'You have to be joking,' Gina said dismissively.

'It's mine,' I said, trying not to sound smug.

They looked at me and I gave a half-hearted shrug that said nothing.

'What the hell did you do for that?' Beth slurred.

'Not much,' I said, 'I just married Edward – the dork!'

'Wait inside'

Di deWolfson

Was his suggestion,
'keep you from the cold'
knowing eyes pacing the street
whipping up a dust of doubt.

She picks a corner, table clothed
in white linen, tensed to the imminence
of wrinkles, crumbs, stray morsels
leering up from livid stains.

In her lap, supplicant fingers bind
in prayer to the God of First Dates
'please please please let this be him'
before the demon behind gritted
teeth, discovering its name, breaks free.

She meets the waiter's old fashioned look
with a look of her own, chosen from
an economy range to match

her new lip gloss,
asks for water, tap, no ice, no lemon
hoping there will be no charge.

Her watch, deadly beetle, grinds down
on seconds with relentless jaws.
In her gut minutes churn into a
curdling mass, garnished with
crimson shreds of rage.

She occupies herself, estimating the
flammable potential of empty red plush,
calculating the trajectory of candles
against the speed of intervention.

Outside, she dares the paving slabs
to keep their faces straight,
count her tears useful as rain
to sluice another Friday night
down the drain.   Yes

The Advisor's Atonement

Paul Chiswick

For the best part of thirty years, I have taken my lunch at this table adjacent to the large Georgian window in the Penny Black café, never once feeling uncomfortable seated among friends, clients, acquaintances. Three generations of them have stepped through my office door: shaking my hand, asking my advice, listening to my suggestions, making their investment choices. Some have done very well: expanded businesses, garnered wealth, taken early retirement. Rarely have I disappointed or given cause for complaint.

Good fortune has laid a kindly hand upon me: a palatial house on a broad, sycamore-lined road in the most desirable area of the city; a devoted young wife to care for me in my old age; two boys and a girl, all grown, all doing well: Rajvir an oncologist, Balkar a solicitor, Jasmeet playing with genes in Cambridge.

What else could you possibly wish for in this life, Dilpreet? you may be tempted to ask.

Forgiveness, I would reply without hesitation. Forgiveness.

People have believed in me for years without question: Dilpreet Dandiwal, a man of peerless reputation and unquestionable honesty. To them, I float above the earth, their all-seeing guru, reading their futures as if they were written down clearly on some magic scroll.

If only it were so.

My nose warned me trouble was on its way. I could smell it: a sulphurous stink leaking from the dealing rooms of the investment banks. I should have warned my clients of the looming financial crisis, counselled them to show prudence and batten down the hatches. I should have. Instead, I chose to hide behind those weasel words of my profession; words my clients always filter out like unwelcome white noise.

Remember, investment values can go down as well as up and you may get back less than you originally invested.

I anticipated what would follow. They accused me of betraying them, their reasoning predicated on the simple fact that I, a man who deals daily with financial giants, am a party to their machinations; that I am "in the know". Ha! If I were I would be living in a palace in the land of my ancestors, the sun beating down on me, the perfume smell of jasmine in my nostrils, not here where the rain thrashes my windows and cold wraps its fingers around my aching joints. Why could they not understand that I, too, have lost money? No matter how many times I pointed this out to them their ears remained closed. What should I have done? Changed my Bentley for a Ford? Sold the villa on Lake Como? Flailed myself in public?

As deepening troubles outlawed the headlines, I toyed with the idea of changing my immutable routine, stop taking my lunch in the Penny Black. Then I thought the better of it. Everyone would consider my absence an admission of guilt or worse, failure.

So here I sit, head held high, waiting to be served. Waiting. Waiting.

Oscar Demeritus, the proprietor, hands iced to his thighs, pins me with narrowed eyes. Short term borrowing from established institutions: not bad, could be worse.

The best rate you can, Dilly. Cash is king in this business.

I know exactly the place, Oscar.

He will survive the downturn - if he continues to pay interest on the huge loan I arranged for him.

At the table next to mine retired couple Hazel and Barry Connor glare daggers. A fair-sized share portfolio, FTSE-100 based.

We're looking for steady growth, Mister Dilpreet. In five years' time we plan to use the money to take a round-the-world cruise.

No problem, Hazel. I would recommend . . .

They will need to be patient. Very patient.

Then Jack Hunter, a barrel-chested, fierce-browed builder steps through the door. My stomach clenches. Jack, a noted big spender, insisted upon a high-risk strategy for his money.

Stuff caution, mate! I hear these BRIC lot are where the money's at.

Far too risky, Mister Hunter. I would counsel we stick with European investments.

Jack is not a man who takes kindly to argument, but in the end, after a great deal of discussion, he deferred to my judgement. The commission I made sufficed to pay for a holiday in Mauritius. If the markets continue to spiral downwards it will break him. The gods help me. He will snap my old bones like dried twigs.

My clients do not fully understand what they let

themselves in for. How could they? It would take me all my waking hours to wade through convoluted clauses drafted by Einsteinian brains. At one time I could grasp all the twists and turns, follow the labyrinthine thread. That time passed long ago. Now I barely trouble to read the words and stumble blindly in the inky fog. Perhaps I should have retired when my mind screamed for rest and my eyes began to play tricks on me, but how can I give up a business that brings me so much in return?

Melanie Demeritus slouches at the edge of my table, weight on one leg, disgust written on her teenage face. A tight black skirt barely covers her teenage backside and I notice a tomato sauce stain on the front of her white blouse. She informs me her father says he would prefer it if I left his café. I firm my jaw and request the menu. She stares at me as if I might be ET and for a brief instant I am tempted to fish out my mobile and phone home, because at this precise moment that is exactly where she wants me to be.

She shrugs, wiggles back to the counter.

I drum fingers on the table. Waiting. Waiting.

The Connors rise from their table; mutter as they pass by. They open the café door and step out into the street, a whiff of distrust trailing them.

After so many years I would miss the cafe. Paintings by local artists hang on pastel walls. Scrubbed wooden tables, each decorated with a slim glass vase containing a single red rose, its efflorescing fragrance mingling with the aroma of hot food drifting in from the kitchen. Simple, homely. A place where my clients and I used to talk easily about matters that concerned us. Would

Aston Villa or Birmingham City face relegation this season? Is Star City a success, or simply a short-term wonder? Isn't it about time Broad Street became safe to walk in an evening, without drunken females heaving their stomach contents over the pavements?

Now, only unkind words slither on their bitter tongues.

Dilpreet Dandiwal. *Devious. Deceptive.*

Why did I behave as I did? A little history may soften your heart and help you to walk in my shoes.

My parents – Amma's stomach swollen with me, a child conceived during a steamy monsoon - came to this country in the year Lee Harvey Oswald blew away President Kennedy. Filled with hope and a young couple's longing they sought a life that would have eluded them had they remained in India. They followed an unmarried cousin on the trail of dreams - Bombay to Birmingham. I do not remember much of my early years, simply a handful of images: sitting cross-legged round a low table, picking with fingers at fish and lentils served with rice in the manner of the land left behind; Amma in her cupboard-sized kitchen preparing enough food for a siege, smells of spices leaking out; Babu reading for the umpteenth time one of the half-dozen books he had brought with him from India; endless conversations of cousins and cricket.

He never mastered English, Babu. He clung desperately to the tongue of his ancestors. Not out of pride or loyalty, but through fear of public mockery. He made do with a nod, a shake of the head, a manic jabbing of the fingers and a plethora of dubious gestures. Amma would have been more comfortable with the alien tongue, but he never allowed her to try and she never went against him. Though he came to a country where women drive cars, wear trousers, and go out to work, he insisted on Amma remaining true to the traditions of a Punjabi wife: cooking and looking after the home. As I grew, I straddled two worlds. An English one; bullied, bemused, beware. An Indian one: cosseted, confused, confined.

At school, my stuttered words and strange skin singled me out. I dreaded the constant finger-pointing and face-pulling of my classmates and their laughing at Amma as she stood at the school gate wrapped in her colourful sari, bright against the industrial greyness of the Midlands sky, holding my snack box containing child-sized samosas and barjees.

Was it simply a matter of learning new words, arranging them in order, pronouncing 'v' correctly? Ha! I had never used a knife and fork, never eaten food unflavoured with spices. I had a mountain to climb, but I persevered. Then at fifteen I learned new words: accomplice, conniving, vodka, marijuana, expulsion. Accomplice: one Wilbert Harrison, sixteen, Afro-Caribbean lineage, son of the local Methodist minister. Conniving: wagging school and finding myself in a dingy, empty house on the fringes of Small Heath. Vodka: a clear, colourless, but mind-numbing liquid imbibed in same house. Marijuana: a sense-heightening and illegal substance, courtesy of Stanhope Roberts, Wilbert's second cousin. When mixed with vodka leads to unpredictable behaviour. Expulsion: what happens when your headmaster learns you have torched the art room, stoned out of your mind.

That was the first time Babu raised his hand to me. It was not to be the last.

I met Josie, a post-punk, looking for a new notch on her tally stick. Short skirt; rubber bracelets; bleached, ragged hair: a boy magnet. She called me "my Indian Prince" and we started dating secretly. Babu spotted us wrapped tightly around each other, lips stuck fast like a barnacle to a rock. He fired a barrage of words, tore me away from Josie and let fly.

From then on our home became a war zone. Except it lacked a no-man's land. The final straw came when Babu forced a plane ticket into my hand.

What's this?

A one-way ticket to Bombay. I have arranged for you to stay with your Aunt Esha in Pune.

But I've never met Aunt Esha! Why are you doing this to me, Babu?

Because, my son, it will help you to remember your roots, rediscover your manners and cleanse your diseased soul. And there will be a wedding. I have found a suitable bride for you, the daughter of an old friend of mine. I trust you will honour my wishes.

You can go to hell!

I threw the ticket at him and left, anger boiling over. The next day I returned to tell my parents I intended to leave home. A small crowd of neighbours stood outside the flat, staring through the open door. I saw Babu slumped in his chair, a man I did not recognise standing over him, shaking his head, Amma holding her hands over her mouth. Then she let out a cry, a terrible wail. It echoed round and round the walls.

For the first time in my life guilt crept up on me, whispered in my ear that I had a duty to Amma and to the father I had disappointed. I knew what I had to do. I would make Amma proud of me. No matter what it took.

I have come a long way since then: climbed a greasy corporate pole; reached the top; submitted to the beckoning finger of self-employment. My reputation followed me like a faithful hound. People flocked to my door.

Dilpreet Dandiwal. *Decent. Dependable.*

'Mister Dandiwal. A word.'

Jack Hunter settles his bulk on the chair opposite. Unshaven, dark-eyed, he would make the perfect nasty piece of work in a Hitchcock thriller. He lays his plate-sized hands on the table, straightens his meaty back. 'In a bit of trouble, eh?'

My flesh jellifies. They say retribution comes swiftly. 'I cannot be held—'

His palm, fingers spread wide, severs my sentence.

'Too late for explanations, mate. I want to know what you plan to do about it.'

I have anticipated this moment; have rehearsed my shaky defence over and over.

'I am afraid I cannot be held responsible for what has happened. I did take pains – as I always do – to point out that you may suffer a loss.'

Redness rises in his thick neck. 'A loss? Is that what you call it? Mate, I call it a disaster.'

'All I can do is advise. In the end it is your decision.'

He shakes his head from side to side. 'Oh, yeah,

that's a great cop out. But it won't work see? The key word here is advice. And from what's happened, yours is crap.'

My heart screams I should tell him to lodge a complaint with the Ombudsman, pursue me relentlessly and then take me to court. I would freely admit my negligence, offer him restitution and suffer disgrace. My head says, hey stupid, this uneducated man does not have the nous to take such a course of action. Shrug your shoulders, stare him in the eye, throw his bullying straight back at him.

He leans back, crosses his arms over his chest. 'I've registered a complaint with the Financial Ombudsman Service.'

My heart cheers; my head falls silent, defeated.

I will not contest his claim, or others that will surely follow.

I will pay my dues. Then perhaps, just perhaps, my clients will forgive me.

An Heir for Pemberley

A modern take on classical characters

Elsa Halling

'It was good of Fitz to send the car for us,' mused George Bennet as the sleek dark blue Bentley purred along the country lanes of Derbyshire.

'Well it certainly beats having to take the train and the local bus. There's no way I would have driven up here. Of course, if you hadn't got a speeding ban it would have made life much simpler. We could have been up here two days ago,' Alicia, his wife replied tartly. George grunted.

'But even that wouldn't have mattered if Liz hadn't had the baby early and so quickly. We could just have popped down to the St Mary's to see her and the new heir to Pemberley.'

'That would have saved us all a lot of trouble,' George conceded.

'I still can't believe she had him at home and took only two hours from start to finish with only the local GP in attendance.'

'I can't see what you're so bothered about. Surely it turned out much better for her?' George couldn't understand all the fuss Alicia was making. But she was still very put out; she had told everyone that her daughter would be going to St Mary's in London. 'It would have been so much nicer for her to have the baby there, just like the Duchess of Cambridge,' she said, 'then they would have come to Longbourn for a few weeks.' Her plans had been foiled and she still felt peeved. Alicia had been so looking forward to Liz coming to stay with them and being able to show off her latest grandson to all her friends, particularly her sister Emily. She had pictured her sister visiting them at Longbourn and sighing enviously over baby Alexander Fitzwilliam in his *Clair de Lune* swinging crib with the powder blue drapes and quilt she had bought from Harrods. She had planned a series of dainty afternoon teas which she would give to her friends and relatives who came to visit the latest addition to the Bennet family. Even being whisked straight up to Pemberley by Fitz's chauffeur just two days after the birth was little compensation for the pleasure of having Liz and the baby down at Longbourn.

George had heard all this before, several times. 'Well don't go saying anything of that to Liz or Fitz, it's *their* baby and I'm sure they are very happy not to have had to go trundling down to the smoke. Whose idea was St. Mary's anyway? I seem to think it came from you originally.'

'It was just a suggestion I made,' Alicia remarked, 'Lizzie and Fitz didn't *have* to agree.' Privately George knew what a fuss there would have been had their daughter not conceded to her mother's suggestion, but was saved from having to reply as they arrived at the gates of Pemberley. The chauffeur slowed down, pressed a button on the shiny walnut dashboard and the great wrought iron gates of Pemberley Park swung silently inwards.

'Oh Fitz it's so lovely to see you,' gushed Alicia as her son-in-law emerged from the great front door of Pemberley and strode down the steps to greet them. He embraced her warmly, then took George's hand in a firm grasp.

'Had a good journey up here, it wasn't too tiring I hope?'

'It was fine, Fitz, thanks to the Bentley and Simmons' driving. It was very good of you to do the honours.' George beamed broadly at his son-in-law.

'It was the least I could do under the circumstances; Master Alexander being in such a hurry rather spoilt all our plans.'

He led them inside the hall, 'Liz is asleep at the moment and so is his little lordship. We'll have some tea and Simmons will take care of your bags.' Alicia tutted to herself; a frown crumpled her face as she struggled to conceal her impatience; she had travelled all this way to see her daughter and new grandson and yet still had to wait.

'It's a lovely afternoon, we'll have tea in the conservatory I think, Brenda.' He turned to the housekeeper who had quietly emerged from behind the green baize door that led to the kitchen area. 'Would that suit you Alicia, or would you like to freshen up first?'

'I'm dying of thirst so tea would be just lovely,' Alicia assured him. If she could have sneaked upstairs and taken a peek at her sleeping daughter and grandson she might have taken advantage of the Pemberley facilities, but she knew very well that Brenda would have shown her into the visitors' downstairs cloakroom, so there was no chance of a quick preview.

Fitz led them through the small drawing room and into the conservatory beyond where they could enjoy the view of the magnificent gardens and waterfalls of the estate.

Alicia had consumed two cups of Lapsang Souchong and a slice of Brenda's excellent Victoria sponge before there was a tap at the door.

'Mrs Darcy's awake now, Sir, she says she's ready for visitors.' The speaker was a new addition to the Darcy household - the nanny who had been engaged to look after baby Alexander.

'Thank you Zoe,' Fitz nodded to the young woman while Alicia eyed her keenly. She seemed barely out of her teens. Alicia hoped she had been properly trained and knew what she was doing. The beige uniform was very professional looking. 'Not a Norland nanny then?' she questioned Fitz when the girl had barely left the room.

Fitz smiled, 'No, not a Norland nanny, Alicia, but she came highly recommended by a good friend of ours who lives in Buxton. She looked after Susie when their son was born. She's fully trained and very efficient. She'll take good care of Lizzie and Alexander.'

Fitz led his in-laws upstairs and into the main bedroom. Alicia could hardly contain her impatience; 'I just can't wait to see the little fellow, can you George?' George was almost nonchalant about the whole affair; this wasn't their first grandchild after all, the Bingleys had two already and small babies held little interest for him. He would be more engaged with the next generation when he could show them his library with its fine collection of first editions, and discuss philosophy with them. Though that pleasure was still a long way in the future; sticky little fingers and valuable books were not compatible. However, Liz had always been his favourite and he knew he must appear to take an interest in his latest grandchild.

Liz was lying in a large four poster bed propped up on pillows, she held her arms out to her mother, 'It's so good to see you Mummy, I'm sorry we messed up all your plans.' Alicia kissed her daughter then looked around for the crib.

'Where's Alexander?' She had pictured Liz lying with the baby in her arms.

'He's still asleep next door. We'll go and take a peep in a minute if he doesn't wake up soon. It's almost time for his feed anyway.'

George hugged his daughter, 'Well done Lizzie,' he congratulated her and kissed her warmly on her cheek. 'We'll leave you and your mother to have a natter and I'll come back when the little fellow is awake.'

The two men made their escape downstairs and George was soon telling Fitz all about his latest acquisition, a set of antiquarian books. Fitz, as ever the perfect gentleman, listened attentively and gave every indication of being suitably impressed by his father-in-law's purchase.

Meanwhile Alicia was extracting all the details of the confinement from her daughter. 'You were so brave darling, when it all happened so quickly, and wasn't it lucky that that Doctor Langley was available. I thought you were going to have one of those block thingy anaesthetics, wasn't it terribly painful for you, sweetheart?'

'You mean an epidural - no there wasn't really time for that. Actually, the midwife came with Doctor Langley and she gave me some gas and air when I needed it.' Liz pushed back the bedclothes and swung her legs to the floor, 'let's go and have a look at him, Mummy, I'm sure you're dying to see him.'

She led her mother to the adjoining room which was really Fitz's dressing room. 'We're using this room as a nursery for now, while I'm feeding him through the night, it's more convenient.'

'Can't the nanny do that; it's what she here for isn't it?'

Liz laughed, 'Course she can't Mummy, she's not a *wet* nurse.' Alicia was taken aback.

'You mean you're feeding him yourself, you know what....' Liz smiled at her mother's obvious discomfort. 'Yes, Mummy, I'm *breast* feeding him, it's so much better for babies, gives them lots of immunities that bottle-fed babies miss out on.'

'I know all that darling, but it's so restricting, you'll be tied up for months, having to be on hand all the time - and think of your figure. I couldn't have done it, not with the five of you!'

Lizzie smiled to herself as Alicia stared round at the décor. 'It's a bit plain darling; I wouldn't have used *grey* in a baby's room.'

'Fitz chose it when we redecorated, it's Farrow and Ball's *Elephant Breath,* isn't that a wonderful name? It conjures up images of those great animals plodding along in the early morning mist. It's perfect for a dressing room.' Alicia wrinkled her nose; Lizzie always had had a vivid imagination. Before she could comment Lizzie continued, 'I'll show you the proper nursery in a minute, you'll like that.' They tiptoed over to the Moses basket on its stand and Alicia had her first view of the heir to Pemberley. She saw a rather red screwed up little face, then slowly the eyes opened and the baby stared solemnly at his grandmother.

Alicia forgot about her displeasure at the colour of the paint, 'Oh Liz darling, he's quite perfect, I do believe he's got Fitz's nose, and all that blond hair.'

'Would you like to hold your new grandson while I get ready to feed him?' Liz lifted the baby out of his basket and laid him in her mother's arms. Alicia crooned fondly over him and almost forgave her daughter for spoiling the plans. She was still disappointed, it would have been so lovely to have them both down at Longbourn for a nice long visit. But they wouldn't have to delay long; he must come down while he was small enough to fit into that expensive cradle. Perhaps she should get a pram for him too, and made a mental note to research the possibility of getting a lovely coach-built one if they were still made. She could picture herself wheeling him around the village, showing him off to all her friends. Lizzie and the baby would stay for several weeks so that she would have the chance to get to know her grandson and Lizzie could have a good rest. She supposed the nanny would have to come as well. Still there would be plenty of room for her now

***

The three days passed all too quickly for Alicia. She had enjoyed lots of cuddles with her newest grandson, but he was a very placid baby and there was little opportunity for extended contact with him. She rather hoped that Liz and Fitz would press them to stay longer, but no such offer was forthcoming. George, however, was not anxious to prolong the visit; he'd done his fatherly duty and was keen to get home again. Relaxing in the back of the Bentley once more he thought about the set of books waiting for him at home and began planning how to rearrange his library shelves in order to accommodate them. Alicia took out her digital camera and flipped through the photos she had taken of her grandson, impatient to get them onto Facebook for all her friends to see.

***

It was as well Alicia was safely in the car and unable to hear the conversation between her daughter and son-in-law.

'Whew I'm glad that's over,' sighed Liz with relief as the Bentley disappeared from view. 'Mummy is such a fuss pot; you'd never believe she'd had five babies of her own. Poor love, she's so disappointed not to be able to show him off to all the friends and family down in Longbourn.' She made a wry face. 'I expect I'll have to take him down before too long as I've already sabotaged her plans.'

Fitz put his arm round her, 'Hardly *sabotaged* darling. It wasn't your fault, though I think Alexander did us a big favour by being in such haste or you'd have had to endure weeks of that down at Longbourn.'

'Oh no I wouldn't, I'm afraid I was a bit naughty.' Fitz raised his eyebrows in puzzlement.

'I never had any intention of going to St Mary's or staying at Longbourn, but you know what Mummy's like, so I told everybody that my due date was three weeks later, and kept my fingers crossed.'

'But surely Doctor Langley had to know, and you could have shared it with me!' Fitz felt suddenly annoyed that she hadn't confided in him.

'No, you're right, Doctor Langley had to be in on the scheme....'

'But not me?' Fitz interrupted in a hurt voice.

'Oh darling, I daren't tell you, we all know you are hopeless at keeping a secret!'

No Plan Made

Kay Howles

We dressed on that cold winter day
And walked down to the lake
To inhale the cold deep in our lungs
Stained by the city's toxic fumes
I remember hugging a kind old friend
I had not seen for years our steamy
Breath swirls round our clinch
I pulled the small boat through
The swelling murky water
Heading for the tall pines
Tilting on the opposite shore
Casting off the snow
The cold watered my eyes
As I stared at her sad face
We were old and grey
And had long forgotten the day
When we had both been young
I held the oars as she tipped
Backwards over the side

A soundless splash a peaceful end
I was alone again and so was she.
Devoid of pain
Agony haunting final years
But silence her respite
From kindness which could never heal
And only bored with low spoke words
From those whose love became charade
But it was I
Who gave the way
Past life to death
With no plan made

Promise

Peter Smerdon

'Tell me about it?'

'What do you mean "it"? Tell you about what?'

'Why don't you begin at the beginning? Tell me how you met Robert?'

'Oh. That's easy. After Mummy and Daddy died, I was very lonely for a while. I just used to mope around the house, never went out. So, my best friend Lisa started to introduce me to men she thought might be...suitable. She used to give dinner parties at her house in Ludlow and sat me next to them. I met Robert that way. He seemed to like me from the first – and I – I certainly liked him.' A long pause. 'I came to love him. He was so charming, and good looking too. Lisa said that he had the right background. Although he wasn't "county", his father had his own solicitor's firm in Bromsgrove and Robert was now running the practice.'

'I know this must be painful for you, but to help you, I need to understand what has happened to you recently. Can you tell me what happened to your par...'

'Help me, help me? You don't want to help me, you're just trying to justify what you're doing to me. You're all the same!'

'Sally, please, I *am* trying to help you. Please stay calm. I believe they died in a car accident?'

'Yes. Yes, that's right. I had just celebrated my twenty-first birthday. We had such a lovely party at our house, Walcott Court, with a marquee on the croquet lawn. It was just magical. Daddy made a beautiful speech, called me his shining princess. I felt as if I was the centre of the world. Then, they drove off the next day to go on holiday – and I never saw them again. They had a head-on collision with a farm tractor on one of the narrow roads close to our house. They were both killed instantly – and the police wouldn't let me see them, said it would upset me. I keep imagining how they must have looked…'

'Sally, thank you for telling me about that. You've talked a bit about your parent's house…'

'*My* house. It's *my* house now.'

'Oh yes, I suppose so – you're an only child, aren't you?'

'Yes, Daddy always said that when I was born, I was so perfect that he and Mummy never wanted any more children.'

'So, back to your house. Can you tell me a bit about it?'

'It's a lovely house. It's been in our family for over two hundred years. It gets a mention in Pevsner. He says "Wallcott Court is a perfect example of a fortified manor house with a moat." It has some very unusual features.'

'Thank you for telling me about the house. Shall we stop there? I'll see you again tomorrow.'

***

She gazed up at him in the velvety gloom. She felt warm, safe and loved – and above all, her whole body felt as though every nerve ending was being caressed and cajoled into pleasure. He lowered his face and kissed her, then moved his lips as far down her arched body as he could reach, continuing to move rhythmically, slowly, deeply...

'Promise you'll never leave me,' she whispered.

He raised his head.

'What did you say?'

'Promise you'll never leave me. Say it – please say it.'

He looked at her for a moment, his head to one side, quizzical.

'OK, I promise,' he muttered.

'I promise I'll never leave you. Say that.'

He sighed. 'I promise I'll never leave you. There, happy now? Can we concentrate on the matter in hand?'

He grinned at her, that lovely heart-stopping grin, and increased the tempo of his movement.

***

'How long were you going out with Robert?'

'What do you mean, "were" going out?'

'Well, Robert seems to have disappeared. I thought you knew that?'

'He hasn't disappeared. He promised never to leave me. I don't know what you're talking about!'
[Subject appears to become distressed]

'OK, let's leave that for the moment. I'd like to hear what happened after you first met Robert.'

'Well, as I said yesterday, we met at a dinner party. Then we did all the usual things together: parties, balls, riding, theatre, concerts. It was just like a fairy tale. All my friends were *so* jealous, especially as Robert had been out with some of them before me – and he'd never loved any of them like he loved me. Eventually, Robert was spending more time at my house than at his. I started to make plans for our engagement and wedding.'

'When was it that Robert asked you to marry him?'

'Oh, he hadn't actually got around to asking me. It was just.... an understanding between us.'

'Do you remember what happened when you went to your friend Lisa's wedding?'

'Well I'm sure we had a lovely time – but I can't remember anything specific. Am I supposed to?'

'We? Did you go with Robert?'

'Well of course I went with Robert.'

'Other people at the wedding report that you arrived in his car – but on your own.'

'That can't be true – he didn't like me driving his car, he was very precious about it. I used to tease him that he loved it almost as much as he loved me.'

'OK, let's put that to one side for the moment. Do you remember what happened when Lisa and her husband cut the wedding cake?'

'No.'

[subject appears to become tense]

'Are you sure? Please try for me, I need to understand what happened.'

'Please don't make me remember.'

[subject starts to cry]

'OK, we'll stop there. I'll call for the nurse to take you back to the ward.'

***

She loved the weekends when Robert stayed over from Friday night until leaving for work on Monday morning.

They spent a lot of time in bed and in between, she cooked meals for them both in the kitchen. Robert used to disappear into her father's wine cellar and "rescue" a bottle for them to drink.

The weekend of Lisa's wedding, she thought he was acting a little strangely. When he arrived on Friday evening, he seemed tired and tense. He snapped at her when she asked him about his day. She took his hand and led him to her bedroom and he seemed to relax. However, once they had made love, he didn't lie with her in his arms, as usual. He got up, saying he was hungry, could she cook him something while he went for a shower?

She used the bathroom, then put on jeans and a t-shirt. She went down to the kitchen, prepared a salad to accompany some fillet steak, opened a bottle of red wine and sat drinking a glass whilst she waited for him to appear. She thought about the dress she had bought for tomorrow's wedding – Robert hadn't seen it yet and she hoped he liked it. She thought of it as her "proposal" dress. She blushed to remember the hints she had dropped, that she would like to go to the wedding with an engagement ring on her finger.
Robert appeared at the door. He had a sullen look on his face – this was a look she was seeing more frequently – and it frightened her.

'I've got something I need to tell you,' he began.

***

'How are you feeling today? Are you ready to tell me what happened at Lisa's wedding?'

'I feel fine – but why do you want to hear about

Lisa's wedding?'

'Well, something very unpleasant happened there. Something that I'm afraid involved you. Do you remember going up to Lisa and her husband as they were cutting their cake?'

'No, I don't remember that.'

'I'm going to show you some photographs – perhaps they will help jog your memory. Whilst the incident took place, the wedding photographer continued to take photographs. I think you might find some of these upsetting.'

'Why should I find them upsetting?'

'Well, you might. Let's start with this one. Do you recognise the three people in this one?'

'Yes, of course, do you think I'm silly? That's Lisa and her husband – and that's me.'

'Can you see what you have in your hand?'

'It looks a bit like….a bit like a knife.'

'You're right, it is a knife. In fact, it's the special knife that Lisa was about to use to cut her cake. I'm now going to show you some photographs of Lisa taken by the police in the hospital, after the event. I warn you, they aren't very nice.'

'Oh God, that's horrible, what has happened to her face? What are they, stitches?'

'Yes, they're stitches. Lisa needed nearly a hundred stitches in her face after the attack. She will be spending a lot of time with the plastic surgeon.'

'But who would do that to her? Poor Lisa.'

'Let me show you this photograph, taken during the attack, before anyone could stop it happening. Do you

recognise this person with the knife?'
[subject screams]

***

The doorbell rang and Jenny went to answer it. She opened the heavy wooden door of the converted farmhouse to her friend, Felicity, who was expected for coffee.

'Hi Jenny!'

'Hello Felicity, lovely to see you, do come in.'

The two women, old friends, kissed on the doorstep, taking care not to disturb each other's immaculate grooming.

When they were settled at the table in the kitchen with fresh coffee, Jenny could see that Felicity had something to tell her. She had that look on her face, the "pregnant cow" look, as Jenny privately described it. There was something inside her that just had to come out.

'Come on then, what is it? I can read you like a book; you've obviously got some gossip for me.'

'Am I that obvious?' smiled Felicity. 'Have I got some gossip for you. But you mustn't tell a soul, it's come from Rupert via the Chief Constable.' Rupert was Felicity's husband and rubbed shoulders with the great and the good in the county.

She settled down in her chair, almost writhing in anticipation of the shock she was about to deliver.

'You remember what happened at poor Lisa Ross's wedding last year?'

'Of course – I was there. It was terrible - Sally Marsh-Ackland ran amok with the cake knife and made a terrible mess of Lisa's face. I shall never forget the screams and the blood all over the white cake icing. It looked just like someone had poured a jar of strawberry purée over it, cascading from the top tier down to the bottom.'

'That's right. And of course, Sally is now being held in Rampton Hospital – at Her Majesty's pleasure, as they say. It was thought that Sally had been dumped by her boyfriend, that rather smarmy solicitor from Bromsgrove. That sent her crazy.'

'Oh yes – but didn't the boyfriend disappear?'

'Right again – he was never seen again.' Felicity paused dramatically. 'Until now!'

Jenny leaned forward in her chair. 'You mean, he's turned up after all this time?'

'In a manner of speaking, dear.' She sipped her coffee. She meant to prolong the suspense as long as she reasonably could.

'You know, of course, that Wallcott Court has been sold. The new owners – I believe the husband is a hedge fund manager – have been undertaking some extensive renovations. Rupert tells me that the builders were in the process of digging out the wine cellar to make a swimming pool, when they came upon a secret, deeper chamber, set in the floor of the wine cellar. Rupert says it's an oubliette.'

'What's an oubliette?' asked Jenny.

'Rupert tells me that it's a dungeon into which prisoners were placed – and just 'forgotten' about. That's what "oubliette" means – forgotten place. Guess what – or rather who - was in there?'

Jenny's mouth dropped. 'No. You don't mean....'

'I do. They found a body, which has now been

identified as that of Robert Harfield. The post mortem says that he was alive when he was put into the oubliette and died of dehydration. Traces of a strong sedative were found in his blood. Apparently, Sally's GP had prescribed it for her when she had trouble sleeping after her parents' deaths.'

Jenny's face went ashen. 'God, that's awful. But who put him in there?'

'Well, we don't know for sure, but the police think it can only have been Sally. There was no-one else in the house that evening before the wedding and Sally came to the wedding in his car. Also, no-one knew about the oubliette. Rupert, who has checked in his own copy, says that even Pevsner doesn't mention it.'

'What a terrible way to go. What can have happened to make that girl do such a horrible thing?'

'Well, my daughter Rosemary, who knew Sally, did say that she was terribly clingy and was always telling anyone who would listen that she and Robert were planning to get married. She also knew Robert a bit and thought that he was just in there for the ride – if you understand my meaning – and that he wasn't serious about the relationship. But, of course, we don't know what she intended – perhaps she just meant to keep him with her. After the assault at the wedding, she ended up heavily sedated for quite a while and then she was committed to Rampton – so poor Robert may just have become – what do they say? – collateral damage.'

The Doctor's Graveyard

Mike Watkinson

The ringing woke him instantly. Fumbling with the handset he croaked, 'Armitage.'

'Dr Armitage, it's Mark here. I need your help. We're having problems with a nineteen year old student admitted five hours ago with a one day history of feeling unwell, headache and a rash appearing on his limbs and spreading. He's deteriorating with a falling blood pressure and his heart rate's up to one hundred and ten.'

'Have you given him antibiotics?'

'Yes, around midnight.'

Henry Armitage glanced at the bedside alarm clock. The display flashed onto 02:17.

'Good God, why not on admission?'

'We were busy on the other ward and…'

'How much fluid has he had?'

'Coming up to a litre, quite a lot.'

'Mark, that's not enough if his BP's falling. Give him another litre of saline over the next hour and I'll be with you in twenty minutes.' They discussed the case in more detail as the consultant searched for fresh clothes. By now his wife was awake.

'You don't often go in at this time,' she said, 'it must be serious.'

'It sounds like septicaemia,' he muttered, 'and I think we've been a bit slow starting treatment. I hope it's not too late.'

Three hours later Henry Armitage looked out of the intensive care unit's window over the city. The first pale streaks of dawn were showing; in the streets below, early morning traffic was starting. He turned back towards the junior doctor with him. He looked frightened, haggard and so very young and vulnerable.

'Mark, it's a terrible disease, and if you haven't seen an episode like that before, let me tell you … it happens. I'm sorry.'

'But you think he should have had his antibiotics sooner, more fluid, more support. I should have done that.'

'Maybe, but I wasn't here, and there is a difference between what I think and what can be achieved.'

'I feel so guilty,' he stuttered, tears trickling down his cheeks, 'it's my fault he died.'

Henry looked at him, thinking what to say next, and made his decision. He gave him some tissues for his tears and took him to one side in the staff room.

'Mark, I'll make some coffee. Can you find us a couple of comfortable chairs in a quiet corner?'

While he made the coffee, Henry's mind drifted back to when he was seventeen and living in Germany. Much of his life there was now just a blur, but he remembered one October weekend. Initially it was much like any other. Not much to do. Nowhere to go. No money to spend. The weak Rhineland sun barely penetrated the mist. He'd been one of a motley gang of Scandinavians, Germans, Dutchmen and Brits living in a hostel. They were hanging around its entrance when Herr Stein the warden came past. He'd trodden on Dieter's foot.

'Entschuldigen Sie, bitte, dass Ich mein fuss unter Ihnen gestossen haben.' quipped Dieter ruefully, rubbing his ankle. Herr Stein had paused, looked round, his face fierce, craggy with dark crevasses worn into his forehead by time and anxiety. He'd slid his steel-rimmed glasses down from his heavy eyebrows. He'd coughed, exhaling smoke and took his Disque Bleu cigarette into his nicotine-stained fingers. Examining it carefully, he'd spoke with a guttural, irritated voice, scarcely looking at Dieter.

'Natürlich, Sie haben mir keine schade getan.' Then, he'd turned and walked away, his broad shoulders swaying slightly with his limp, before he disappeared into the unkempt sodden shrubbery and the mist. Silently we watched him go. No birdsong, but in the distance the boom of foghorns of the Rhine barges as they ploughed unceasingly north and south along the great river.

'What was all that about?' asked Jens, a Swede whose German wasn't up to speed.

'Dieter jokingly apologized for putting *his* foot under Stein's,' explained one of the Dutch guys, 'and Stein replied that he hadn't done him – Stein - any harm! He's a strange man, an enigma. Difficult to know what he's going to do, how he'll respond to something.'

'What's he like to work for, Dieter?'

'I've been his assistant for two months. He's in a lot of pain sometimes, I think. His hip bothers him; it's a war wound. When the pain's bad, he can be short tempered, but I like him. He really cares about the men in the hostel – even you guys, though I don't know why! And usually you can tease him.'

'I've got the chairs' said Mark loudly, 'and you look a million miles away! The kettle's long boiled!'

'Sorry! I'll make the coffee then let's sit down. I was thinking of when I lived in Germany. And that is relevant to today. I was seventeen and lived in a hostel with Dave, another English student. We were there on a sort of reconciliation mission, if that's not too grand a word. Most of the thirty guys living in the hostel were Germans who had been orphaned in the war, their parents killed when they were children. Through their late teens and early twenties, this had been their home. They lived two to a room in clean but not very luxurious conditions and apparently many of them had become quite nationalistic. Not the right thing in post-war Germany! Then someone had the bright idea that they needed to mix with other nationalities, including the English, to dilute some of the ideas they still had about being German. That's what Dave and I were doing there for six months between school and university. Being English! Not always easy. England beating Germany in the World Cup Final that year was one of the hardest times we had. Several guys in the hostel stopped speaking to us and Dave got roughed up in Köln one night.'

'And that's pretty much how we lived our lives. Lived with the Germans in the hostel. Local bars and dances on Friday and Saturday nights. Church on Sundays. The six months passed pleasantly and unremarkably. And, yes, I think the German guys in the hostel eventually came to see we were pretty much like them, which was probably as much as we could hope to achieve. Except one day, Herr Stein, the warden of the hostel, took me aside after church and spoke in English for the first time. Before that I'd thought he couldn't speak English at all.'

'Henry, we go on a walk at three o'clock,' he said, gesticulating at his watch and pointing at the three. It wasn't a suggestion. I was so amazed by this approach, all I could do was nod in agreement. We met after lunch by the entrance of the hostel and Herr Stein led the way.

'Good, komm!' he set off in his swaying, limping gait. We walked along mundane village streets heading towards the Rhine autobahn bridge. The buildings were new post-war developments, smart estates of houses with dormer window bedrooms in the roofs and immaculately kept front gardens with clipped evergreen shrubs fencing off the pavements. Few people were about and even fewer cars. Although the wind was southerly, it was blowing Alpine ice up the wide valley and flood plain. For some minutes, nothing was said, but finding the silence difficult, I blurted out 'Bad leg?' and then blushed at my ineptitude. To my surprise Herr Stein turned round momentarily, grinned, said 'Shitty leg!' and laughed. He slowed his pace and we walked more side by side. He took off his glasses and polished them on his wool scarf, at the same time gazing into the distance.

'Before the war, life was not easy in Germany. My father worked long hours on a farm. I was one of eight children, and after my youngest sister was born my mother nearly died. We were poor. Two of my brothers died. Even when I was fifteen in 1926 I could see that my father was slowing down; he could not look after us forever even though his children worked with him in the fields. The farm was not the answer for a growing family. Can you understand me?'

'Your English is very good.'

'Thank you. So as soon as I had grown a little more I left home. I had already been in the Hitler Jugend or Youth as you would call it, so at sixteen it was easy to get into the army. I was a good soldier and by the start of the war I was the head of a group of tanks.'

'A Tank Commander.'

'Ja.' He coughed. 'I was on the Russian front and there I was injured, hit in the bone in the hip. Perhaps I was lucky because I was taken back to hospital. I cannot remember much. I was ill for months with a fever and wound infection and now I have this shitty leg but I'm alive. Soon after I left my tank, a Panther, it broke down and all my men were burnt alive inside it by the Russians.' He stood, looking at his cold bare hands, the thick calloused fingers betraying years of labour somewhere far from an office desk. I waited and eventually he sighed, looked up, took his bearings and said, 'We're almost there.'

We walked on in the fading light and came to a simple double wrought iron gate with high Leylandii trees on both sides. Beyond this the trees bordered a dog-leg drive.

'Komm.'

The driveway was eerie in the gloaming but we rounded a corner to see hundreds of eternal lights with their candles burning, flickering red in their glass bowls. They were but dim footlights to occasional dark figures knelt by or bent over graves, tending and tidying them, leaving fresh flowers and lighting new candles. Behind them Leylandii again formed a curtain of deep green with the threatening steel-grey sky hung like a theatre backdrop behind them.

'You know this?' asked Herr Stein

'Ein Friedhof, a graveyard, but I've never seen one as beautiful as this in England.'

'Hohen Katholischen Kirche. High Catholic. Let's take a seat.'

Deep in the graveyard, we sat down. He looked around. It was a minute or two before he spoke.

'Unfortunately, I have a graveyard of people I killed in the war.' His voice began to break.

'I'm sorry, what do you mean?'

'I killed many people. I was responsible for many deaths.'

'But you believed you were doing the right thing at the time.'

'No, you're wrong, I didn't. But I was a soldier. I had to obey orders. So I obeyed orders, but I did the wrong thing and killed people, God forgive me.' He leaned forward and held his head in his hands. His face was wet. 'This is my graveyard, God forgive me. I can never, never put it right!'

'But you're a good man. I can see that. All of us in the hostel can see that. You try to help us. You do help us. It wasn't your fault. You mustn't despair like this.'

I didn't know what to do. I touched his shoulder, not sure if I should, but I wanted to comfort him and show him I still respected him. He sat there rubbing his eyes, stroking the stubble on his face, slowly controlling himself, slowly pulling himself up. He coughed, blew his nose noisily.

'I'm sorry. Today is twenty four years exactly since my men were killed in the tank. It is always a difficult day. Normally...in the last few years...one of my sons comes with me, he is a little older than you, but this year he has refused and you...you remind me of my son. I'm sorry, das ist ungerecht... unfair. I had wanted to say something different to you.'

'I didn't know that you and Frau Stein had children.'

'Two sons.'

Silence.

'Two sons?'

'Yes, but they don't like me. I was too difficult a father. When I came home after the war, I had bad dreams and a bad temper. I was hard on them. Even now, as you see, it is very distressing to think of my men. And my boys are at university, but they do not come home very often. It's very hard for Gisela.'

We sat there in the fading evening light watching the candles burn ever brighter, each with his own thoughts. Just when I thought he was going to get up and lead us home, he turned to me.

'That other thing I wanted to say to you... I understand that you plan to be a doctor.'

'I hope so. I've got a place at medical school, but there's a lot of examinations to pass first.'

'I'm sure you will do well. You have learned German quickly.' He paused. He spread his arms widely, sweeping across the gravestones in front of us. 'If you do become a doctor, then one day you too will have a graveyard as big as this.'

'What? Me? I don't think so. What do you mean?'

'Every doctor has a graveyard. It is filled with the mistakes he or she has made. Filled with the bodies of those who die under his care, those who might have lived if he had not made a mistake. Or tried a bit harder. Or tried a different treatment, or remembered something that would have helped. That's how a doctor's graveyard is filled.'

'I'm not becoming a doctor to have a graveyard.'

'But you will have one. There will be mistakes.'

I didn't reply. I didn't want that conversation to go on. We got up and walked out of the cemetery. But the idea followed me, nagging, scratching at my mind.

'If I do have a graveyard... then what?'

'Then you must remember all the people you have helped who are walking around in the streets. You will have forgotten most of them, and most of them will not be thinking about you – they may never even meet you, but you will have helped them. There will be far far more of them than are laid in your graveyard. They will not come in your dreams as the dead do. They will not haunt you. Neither will they greet you or thank you. But they will be there, alive, well and happy, thanks to you.'

I couldn't help but smile at his sense of timing as we walked out into a busy street with people walking past us without a glance, as families moved to their Sunday evening destinations.

'So not too big a graveyard,' I said, 'perhaps I could live with that.'

'Not "perhaps"... you will have to. There is no choice. Komm... it's dark. Let's go back.'

'We stayed two more months in the hostel. Herr Stein never spoke to me again.'

Henry Armitage stopped talking. The sun was now over the rooftops, the day was beginning. Mark's tears had dried. He managed a wry smile.

'What a strange story.'

'I don't share it with many people. It's helped me from time to time, perhaps it will help you.'

'What happened to Herr Stein?'

'He died of lung cancer six months later. When I heard I wondered if he already knew that he was dying when he talked with me.'

'Do *you* have a graveyard?'

'We're not really here to talk about me, are we, but yes, I have one. I've been a consultant for twenty two years and I'm sorry to say that I add to it some years. Unforgivable mistakes. I become angry and depressed with myself.' He paused and looked at Mark.

'How are you feeling about Mr. Babbington's death tonight?' he asked in a kinder tone of voice.

'Upset and annoyed with myself.'

'Upset I understand. Why annoyed?'

'Because I should have given him antibiotics sooner.'

'Yes, I agree.'

'Oh! I thought you might counsel me not to worry.'

'No, I support your suggestion about the antibiotics. What else might you have done?'

'What else?! I don't know!'

'Then take a moment to think... away from the crisis and the panic.'

'Well, I er... suppose perhaps... more fluids?'

'Yes, I think so too, perhaps even before his blood pressure began to drift. And I think you should have called me sooner, even if it was the middle of the night.'

'Yes, though I thought I would manage.'

'Not this time, I'm afraid, but there are good things there, aren't there, Mark? You know what to do and you'll be able to do them next time. There will be a next time, you know. You're a good doctor. I've worked with you for four months and I'm very impressed by you. You have a good knowledge of medicine for someone at your stage of training. Don't let this episode get you down. We'll talk to the relatives together. It's important they understand just how ill he was when he was admitted yesterday.'

'But it was my fault he died, that's why you told me the story.'

'Maybe he would have died anyway. But a doctor like you needs to think about doctors' graveyards and how to face up to them. Remember, we *all* have them.'

'No one has suggested that I think about it in this way before.'

Henry stood.

'Look, the sun's up. We've got an hour before the others arrive. Let's go for a walk and get a breath of fresh air in the streets. Herr Stein would recommend it.'

As they walked in companionable silence, Henry saw some of the weight of the night leave the younger man and a new resolve appear. He wondered how often Mark would quietly re-visit this man's virtual grave in his future years as a doctor.

The Dream

Maggie Cabeza

At number 131 Millenium Way in a bustling town named Oswestry, lived an ordinary family composed of Trish (aged sixteen) and her younger sister Beth (aged thirteen) together with their parents; Frank and Mary. The family had moved there before the girls had started pre-school, so by this age, they had lived a very settled and familiar existence where changes were small and life seemed to flow neatly. Both girls got on well, although they were now getting to the stage when Trish felt she was more of an adult and a little gap was beginning to form between them regarding their interests and friends.

Our main protagonist of this tale is Trish and the essence of the story is the emotional bond between two people that transcends all distance. The possibility of first love, I hear you ask? No, for Trish was actually quite shy and although she felt quietly drawn towards one of the most popular lads in her class, Ryan McNaught, the desires and dreams were more in her mind than in her behaviour around him. The bond was with her grandmother Moira, who lived in France with her Grandad Pete. Their relationship had been mainly nourished by the holidays that Trish and her family had taken in the town of Saint Lo, in Normandy. During these visits, Grandma Moira and Trish talked endlessly and did many things together. Trish loved learning from her; the needlework and patchwork quilts. She would always come back home with small colourful projects completed. She particularly loved the enthusiasm that Grandma shared with her about the excitement of becoming a young woman and venturing out into the world to explore and experience all the wonders that life can hold. Trish felt she too would like to move country as her grandmother had done but was not yet sure where that special place would be; but the mere thought excited her.

Trips to France happened nearly every year. It had been the highlight for the family but the last two years they had been unable to go as overtime had been greatly reduced at the car factory and Frank and Mary had to cut back drastically. Trish inevitably missed that time with her grandmother but kept in touch by writing letters or sending her some small homemade gifts in the post.

One day, Mary approached both girls and said that Grandma was not very well and that she needed to make a trip to stay with her for a few weeks. She explained that there was nothing to worry about but their grandparents did need her support. Trish became a little anxious on hearing this, but was reassured by her mother not to fret. Trish felt a huge urge inside to ask her mother if she could go, but knew that it would be pointless as she had just started sixth form and money was tight.

The few weeks her mother was away dragged and the whole family felt somewhat at a loss without her. Trish automatically did what she could to help out in the house, but deep down she just wanted to keep busy till her mother's return. The day soon came when Mary came home, looking somewhat pale and subdued. When Trish asked her mother how her grandma was, Mary said that she was not very well and had needed to go into hospital. Trish felt a reluctance from her to share what exactly was wrong and thought better to accept it for now. However, this particular night when Trish went to bed weary from the unsettled few weeks, she had a dream. A dream that was so vivid that when she awoke, she felt that it really had happened. So what was the dream? Simply, her grandmother appeared to Trish, sat in a wheelchair. No words were spoken between them. She merely lifted her arms up in the air and Trish just put her arms around her grandmother, her cheek on her grandmother's warm bosom and in that silence the image disappeared. At breakfast, she told her mother of her dream. Mary seemed very taken aback by the dream and Trish went on to explain how hard she was finding it not having that contact with her grandmother, but hoped she would soon.

Sadly this was not meant to be, for her grandmother passed away two days later. Trish and the family were heartbroken and consoled each other in their grief. That evening, as Trish sat on her bed looking at photos of her grandmother, her mother came in to see her.

'What happened mum? What did she die of?' she asked her mother tearfully.

'She died of a brain tumour, love. She just couldn't fight it,' explained Mary.

'Oh Mum!' Trish cried, curling into a ball as her body filled with pain at the thought of her grandmother suffering.

Mary embraced her daughter and rocked her gently. She too was shedding a tear now.

'I know love, it's so sad. But I have something to say to you which I feel is important for you to know.'

Trish leaned back and looked at her mother, her

face red and glistening with tears.

'On the night you had your dream, she had gone into a coma.' Trish looked confused at what her mother was saying.

'Can't you see Trish? She came to say good bye to you. You two have always been so close.'

Trish felt this lift in herself as she recalled the dream and the vividness of the sight and touch of her grandmother.

'Mum, you're right! She did.'

Mother and child then continued to spend time talking and looking at the happy memories captured in the photos spread around her quilt. And that night Trish slept peacefully without dreams, but with a lighter heart.

A week and a half later, the family made the trip to Saint Lo to attend the funeral. When they got to the grandparents' home after the long journey, Mary put the kettle on for some tea and Frank was talking to Grandad Pete in the lounge. Beth was quietly coping with the loss of her grandmother. She had not been as close to her grandmother as Trish, but loved her just the same. Her main unease was about attending her first funeral. Beth asked her mother if she could run a bath and just unwind from the trip. She knew that she could quietly and privately release the tears she was holding within whilst she lay in the steamy water.

Trish walked around her grandmother's bedroom, looking at the little trinkets and photos, recalling memories shared. Little pieces of craftwork they had made together whilst Trish was being taught were displayed on bedside cabinets. Trish then went to the back of the house where there was a laundry room, meaning to go out into the garden. As she turned into the room she froze at the object that stood before her. It was a wheelchair, the one that she had seen in her dream. As the strength returned to her legs, Trish rushed into the kitchen.

'Mum! Come quickly, this is even more proof!'

Mary put the teapot down, adorned with one of grandmother's crocheted covers and followed her daughter.

'Look,' she said, pointing at the contraption. 'I believed it before, Mum, but I believe it *even* more now!'

Her mother took hold of Trish's hand and smiled. 'Dear, I was gobsmacked when you told me your dream, because whilst I was here, Grandma had a stroke. The hospital gave us a wheelchair when she was discharged.'

Trish shook her head in disbelief but also with the contentment that her grandmother's love was so strong that she could not leave without saying goodbye.

H_2O

Di de Wolfson

Most days I forget I am more than half water
imagine that coffee and coke quench my thirst
make excuses for tiredness, ignore dehydration,
take for granted the free flow of body and mind

Still thirsting, I shrug off a very slight headache,
ignore a parched tongue, dismiss cracking lips
deny I feel sluggish, but then it gets harder
can't quite reach the top shelf, I'll have to admit

I've lost something precious, my cells have been shrinking
flexible feelings are thickening to sludge
as channels run dry I get stuck in a low mood,
can't rise to the moment, can't reach quite so high.

At last, being desperate, I reach for a litre
of crystal clear energy straight from the tap,
it floods through my body, sets energies racing
shoals of imaginings brimming with life.

Now every glass stimulates waves in succession

no stopping me now, I'm addicted to wetting
my whistle and blowing it often and loud
in praise of my fifty per cent, H_2O.

The Letter

Maidy Clark

She woke up early with the first hint of butterflies. Jumping out of bed, she went into the bathroom and turned the taps on for a luxurious bath. She had treated herself to some pure Sandalwood essential oil just for this occasion. Such an erotic smell she thought. When she heard the doorbell, she looked out the window and saw the post man below her.

There had been so much mail in the past few days, she was not surprised to see him. Cards had been arriving from people she had forgotten existed. She turned off the taps, grabbed her dressing gown and went downstairs to the door.

'What a lovely morning,' she said as she opened the door.

'Yes,' he smiled back, 'Can you sign here, please.' He gave her his book and pen, then handed her the pile of letters. Taking them from him, she thanked him, closed the door and went into the kitchen. While she waited for the kettle to boil she sorted through the mail, mostly handwritten, a couple of bills, and then the official looking one from the Post Office she had signed for. She turned it over in her hands, curious as to what it might be.

She picked up her cup of tea and the rest of the letters, walked into the sitting room and sat in her chair. It looked over the large formal garden, with bird feeders prominently displayed to amuse her as she drank her tea in the mornings. But today she was engrossed in the mail.

Putting the others aside, she opened the official

Post Office envelope, carefully pulling out a piece of paper, which was folded around another envelope. Putting this second envelope into her lap she read the letter.

It was official. An apology. It explained the enclosed letter had been found behind one of the shelves when they were refurbishing the sorting office. It had taken them a few months to trace her, but now felt sure they had the right person, and were pleased to be of service, even if it was twenty years late.

Josie was intrigued, she picked up the envelope from her lap and turned it over.
Her hand flew to her mouth. In the centre it read, "Josie Spencer, 43 Cumbria Road, Alton, Hampshire", surrounding this were assorted inks which had written other things on it. "Not known at this address." "Try Winchester." "Try Alton Barnes, Wiltshire." But the beautiful scripted writing that bore her name and old address she recognized immediately. Writing she had not expected to see again. So long ago. She thought she had forgotten, but all the pain and feeling came flooding back as she looked down at her name on the envelope.

Her heart finally calmed down. Her right hand held on to the neck of her dressing gown as she stared down at the envelope in her still shaking left hand. She carefully placed the envelope on the coffee table and reached for her cup of tea. Cold. She suddenly remembered the bath. She rose from her chair and went back upstairs. Sitting on the edge of the bath she pulled the plug out and sat watching the water go down the hole. The sudden noise of the last few drops being sucked down brought her back again. She shook her head.

'I must pull myself together. This is ridiculous,' she said out loud.

Wiping the mist from the mirror, she searched for the person she had been all that time ago, but didn't see what she was looking for behind the blue eyes and laughter lines, as she liked to call them. Walking into the bedroom she picked the clothes from the floor and then made the bed. Back in the bathroom again she washed and dressed herself, applied her makeup and combed through her slightly greying hair before pinning it up in its usual bun.

Downstairs she avoided the sitting room, tidying instead the kitchen, washing down all the surfaces unnecessarily. When it was spotless, she put on her rain coat, picked up the car keys and went out the front door.

Sinking down into the hairdresser's chair, she looked to see who she would have today. She gave thanks silently as she saw it was Joan. Joan did not twitter on incessantly. She would ask a few questions, and if there was no response she left the clients to their own thoughts.

'Special occasion, dear?' she asked.

'Yes,' Josie replied.

'Looks as if the rain will hold out.'

'Yes,' Josie replied. Joan gave up.

Josie silently turned over in her mind all the things she still had left to do. The wedding was at three thirty. Joan put the curlers in her hair, and then applied the lotion, all the time Josie was thinking. Staring straight through the mirror.

'Can you sit in this chair now, dear? Do you want any magazines?'

'Thank you.' The hairdresser showed her to a dryer, plonking a pile of magazines in her lap then brought her a cup of tea.

An hour later, her hair washed and set, her face beetroot from the heat of the dryer, she left Joan. Glancing at her watch she hurried on to the florist. Really this was Ben's job, but she knew he wouldn't do it properly. Some button holes and a little posy was all she needed. They should be ready when she got there, then home to rest and dress.

Letting herself into the house, she could hear the phone ring. Leaving the keys in the door she picked it up.

'Hello,' she said.

'Josie?'

'Ben. Is everything alright?'

'Yes, of course. I wanted to hear your voice.'

'I'm fine. Trying to get everything done. I've nearly finished then I can rest before the car gets here. You?'

'I'm fine. Now you go and rest. I want you well rested for this afternoon. See you later. Bye.'

He hung up, not waiting for an answer. So like him. She smiled at the phone, walked into the kitchen to put the kettle on and kicked off her shoes. Then, remembering the keys in the door, went to retrieve them and pick up the box of flowers.

Sitting on the stool, she looked at the posy while she enjoyed her cup of tea. It was pretty. She had chosen dried flowers so it would keep. And the blues of the flowers would match the pale blue of the wedding dress.

The button holes were all red carnations as a stark contrast.

She looked up at the clock. She really ought to eat. It would be tea time before they sat down for the wedding breakfast. And three cups of tea would not sustain her. She opened the fridge, but nothing enthused her with appetite, so closed it again. Opening the larder, she saw the biscuits and decided they would do for now. When it was all over, and the butterflies had died down, she would eat.

Josie decided to have her bath now, and then rest in the lounge for an hour before getting dressed and made up. She'd have to be careful not to let her hair spoil whilst in the bath though. With a start she remembered why she had to have a bath now instead of this morning.

She got off her stool and went into the lounge. She felt a sense of shock that the letter was still on the coffee table where she had left it. Gingerly she picked it up, turning it over once more. No name and address on the back, she supposed that was why the Post Office had tried so hard to find her. They could not send it back to the writer, not unless they opened it. Looking more carefully she could make out some of the date. It was definitely June, and it was 1983. But the actual day was too faded to read. Had it been before the twenty first or after?

She put on her glasses again to have another look. No, it was no good, she could not make it out. If she opened it, she would know. But she did not want to open it. Not today of all days. Walking to the dresser, she opened the drawer, picked up a pile of napkins and placed the envelope under them. She went up stairs to run another bath.

Her dressing gown round her, hair untroubled by the bath, she shakily applied a little makeup. Not too much, but enough to make her feel special. A bit of pink lipstick, and some mascara, and a touch of pale blue eye shadow. She slowly rolled each stocking up, enjoying the sensation, then pushed her feet into the new powder blue shoes. She pulled her new dress over her face with care, and finally put on the matching jacket. The blue of the dress brought out the darker blue of her eyes. She looked herself up and down, smiling at her own reflection. The greying hair could almost be blond, she told herself.

Downstairs in the kitchen she poured herself a vodka, added a slice of lemon and a dash of lemonade, then waited for the car to pick her up. Five minutes to spare. A couple of her friends had offered to pick her up, had even offered to stay the night, but she declined all their kind offers. It was so much easier to do things on your own, loneliness never having been a problem.

She sat back in the seat as the driver pulled away. He had put the button holes on the front seat for her. As she looked out of the window, her mind betrayed her and the thoughts started drifting in once more. Then she had sat next to her father.

Closing her eyes for a few seconds, she heard his voice, and felt the pressure of his calloused hand as it held hers.

'Are you sure this is what you want? It is never too late to change your mind, you know that don't you?' He looked at her as he asked.

'Daddy, of course it is what I want. I love him.'

She returned the squeeze of his hand. And they journeyed to the church in silence.

Josie shook her head to erase the images. She was going to marry Ben now. She felt contented and happy about this. Her father had been dead for twelve years now, but he would have liked Ben, she knew that. Her mother had died when she was just four, so she had no idea if she would have liked Ben or not. Just trusted that she would. He was a good man, and she was lucky to have found him. That was what her friends said. He told her, he was the lucky one. Josie thought they were both lucky. The butterflies in her stomach were reaching fever point. The vodka had hardly touched them.

'We're here darling, are you ready?' Her father asked as the car drew up outside the church.

'Yes,' she smiled back. So excited. She could see people standing outside, and knew inside the church would be full. The driver helped her out of the car, picking up her long white veil. Then she saw Mike approach them, his face unsmiling.

'He's not here yet, can you go around again. I am sure he won't be long.' She had got back in the car, with her father. And they had driven around in silence. Eventually, the vicar suggested that they all go home. Maybe there would be a message for her there. Something had happened to him. But she heard nothing. She never knew why, never saw him again, never heard from him again.

'We're here, Ma'am,' the driver called her back.

'Thank you.'

Getting out of the car, she looked around for Ben. She clutched her posy tight. Their friends were waiting for her. They walked over to her, kissing her cheek, smiling. Teresa took the box of buttonholes.

'Where's Ben?' Josie asked. Teresa shook her head.

'No one's seen him yet. Don't worry. He'll be here, Josie'

The butterflies were dive bombing her abdomen now. She felt sick. Jack walked towards her, hugged and kissed her.

'Here let me give out the flowers. There should be enough for everyone.' Josie reached into the box Teresa held. Taking out one flower at a time, she busied herself, attaching one to everyone's jacket or dress.

Ten minutes passed. Josie felt close to tears.

'Josie, I know Ben, he'll be here,' Teresa assured her.

'Well, should we go inside, or wait here on the pavement?' Josie asked. 'It's not like at a church, is it? Where the bride can't go in before the groom?' Even she could hear her voice crack as she said it.

'Yes, let's get off the pavement, there may be some seats inside,' Teresa agreed as she guided Josie up the steps of the building.

Entering the building, an official looking man approached them.

'Josie Spencer?' he asked the group.

'Yes, that's me.'

'I've a message for you. Mr Thorpe has just

phoned. He is so sorry, but the car broke down. He'll be here as soon as he can. We've assured him that is alright, as yours is the last wedding of the day. He's getting a taxi, and will be here presently.'

Josie felt her body relax. Everything was going to be just fine. There was laughter around her now, instead of whispering voices.

Then she saw him. Running up the steps, panting. Jack his best man, greeted him, slapping him on the back as he shook his hand. She watched as Ben doubled over, trying to catch his breath.

'Nearly got away, then?'

'Nearly.' He winked at Josie. The official came towards them.

'Can I have the bride and groom now?' he called.

Everything went smoothly. Then the official said, 'You are now man and wife, you may kiss each other.' And they did. Josie felt the happiness well up inside, and the butterflies decided to have a rest, as they fluttered to a standstill.

He didn't carry her over the threshold. She told him not to be so silly. They were too old for such things. He tried though. And they both nearly broke their backs. His, lifting her; hers, when he dropped her. But they laughed. Once inside, she felt shy. She pondered; this was daft really, they had practically been living together for two years. But now they really were man and wife. She really was married. Walking through the hallway she looked at her hand, there was the gold band on her finger to prove it.

She thought she would burst with delight.

'There's champagne in the fridge, do you want to open it while I go and get changed out of this? Into something more comfortable.' She grinned at him. Ben winked back.

'Good idea. I'll take it into the lounge. Are you sure you don't mind not going away?' he called after her, as he made his way to the kitchen and she started up the stairs.

A few moments later she came down, in her loose trousers and t-shirt. He was standing by the coffee table, looking through the unopened mail she had left there that morning.

'That's better, now I can relax. And no, I don't mind staying here. I would have told you if I did. You know that.' She took the champagne flute from his hand. They looked at each other and chinked their glasses.

'I love you Mrs. Thorpe,' he said.

'It is strange to have a new name. Josie Thorpe. And this is much better than staying in some stuffy hotel, and having people around us.' She followed him to the settee. They sat close together. He put his arm around her, she leant her head on his shoulder and Ben switched on the TV.

Later, Ben suggested they go to bed to finish watching the film up there.

'You go up, I'll be there in a moment. I just want to tidy up down here,' she said.

Ben went upstairs to the bathroom and she took the empty glasses and bottle into the kitchen. Going back into the lounge, she checked the windows and walked past the dresser. She opened the drawer, lifted the napkins and took out the envelope. She stared at the writing as she walked into the kitchen. Reading the name out loud: 'Josie Spencer.'

She walked up to the pedal bin, placed her foot on the pedal, and ripped the envelope into shreds.

'It's rude to read other people's mail,' she said, watching the pieces fall in the bin.

'Josie, are you alright? You're missing the film,' Ben yelled down the stairs.

'I'm fine. Just fetching another bottle of champagne, Mr. Thorpe.'

About the authors

Mark Bradbury has only recently taken up short story writing. His previous literary experience was a brief, part-time career over a decade ago writing technical articles for magazines. Mark had a regular column and occasional articles in the long-since defunct classic car magazine "Real Classics" and has also published in the still current "Classic American". Mark is now concentrating on developing his fiction writing skills.

Cashel Brook is working hard to improve his writing skills. He is currently working on his first novel which he hopes to complete this summer.

Maggie Cabeza is a counsellor. She loved writing stories at school which she based on her vivid dreams. Reconnecting with her writing and imagination has been rewarding. The group is very welcoming and encouraging. There is always something to take away and explore. She has mainly focused on short stories, but now feels ready to try her first proper novel.

Following two successful careers as a Civil and Structural Engineer, and an Account Manager in the IT industry, **Paul Chiswick** decided to concentrate on improving his writing. Currently, he has three published novels, three non-fiction books and has been included in two anthologies, one of which was as a result of being selected in a national competition. He has enjoyed success with his short stories, often being shortlisted but not yet winning that elusive prize. When not writing he divides his time between helping unpublished authors get into print and promote themselves, and producing living memories from static images. More at www.paulchiswick.com

Award winning author, **Maidy Clark** has been writing stories since she could hold a pen in her hand. After achieving her MA in Creative Writing in 2007, Maidy began tutoring for The Open University on their creative writing modules as well as tutoring at University of Winchester. She has also worked in various male prisons in the UK, teaching creative writing, drama and English Literature.

Dave Griffiths is a retired accountant and is writing a novel set in Liverpool and the USA.

Elsa Halling has been an avid reader since childhood. After retiring from teaching she tried her hand at writing and obtained a Masters in Writing from Warwick University. Essentially a short story writer who enjoys travel, she has been inspired by the people and places encountered on her journeys. She has published a collection of short stories on Amazon Kindle.

Kay Howles has recently published her first novel *Gray's Well* on Amazon. She has been writing for fifteen years and since retiring is getting her various works completed and into print. A member of Balsall Writers for two years, she finds interaction with other authors invaluable for keeping her focussed. *After Gray* and *Gray's End* are under way and she anticipates publication this year.

At the beginning of the new century **Penny McCulloch** decided to indulge her desire to write poetry by taking a Warwick University Open Studies course. Since then she has written sporadically. Some of her poetry is inspired by Christianity and a desire for justice. Other poems tackle issues which have personal significance such as her mother's dementia.

After winning a poetry competition in 1998, **Derek Miller** went back to life in an office and has just recently surfaced to write short stories and poems. He does like to consider the 'what if' scenario in his writings.

Katrina Ritters has been writing creatively for a decade or more and has been part of Balsall Writers group since its inception. After years of travelling up to Sheffield to take an MA in writing she is amazed to find so much creative talent within walking distance of her home. A slowly growing pile of prose and poetry is currently filling up her bottom drawer.

Anne Santos reads, writes and listens to poetry; she is a published author of articles, short stories, poetry and four paperback novels. A change of publisher in 2013 has seen all her books (written under the pen name of Annette De Burgh) now released exclusively on Amazon Kindle and in paperback before becoming available on other e-book platforms. www.annettedeburgh.com

Peter Smerdon has always enjoyed reading a wide variety of genres. Having retired, and in theory with more time available, he is now attempting to create some readable literature of his own, initially with short stories but also with a novel. This is progressing slowly.

Mike Watkinson is a retired doctor. He is currently doing a part-time MA in Writing at the University of Warwick.

Di de Wolfson has been writing complex poetic prose and poetry for many years. Her early influences were Chaucer, Milton, Shakespeare, and the Metaphysical poets, and latterly Ted Hughes, Seamus Heaney, Elizabeth Bishop, and very recently Mark Doty. She is currently studying with Manchester Writing School and teaching poetry and a few of her poems have appeared in anthologies.

Printed in Great Britain
by Amazon.co.uk, Ltd.,
Marston Gate.